Praise for "A Brighter Palette"

"A Brighter Palette is just an all-around enjoyable read that will break your heart one minute and heal it the next but most importantly Brigham has left me hungry for the next installment."

-Padme's Library

"Brigham Vaughn is in a league of her own when it comes to creating characters who come to life on the page. Her writing is smooth and she sweeps me along while her descriptions, both of scenery and of sexy times so vibrant I can almost see the images and feel the caresses.

A Brighter Palette is a well written, captivating and thought-provoking romance. It takes what are huge issues for some people and forces Siobhán and Annie to come to terms with them, in the process forcing the reader to think about the topics in question."

-Marleen Kennedy

"A welcome change from the typical formulaic romance novel. Highly recommend!!"

-Leslie Le

"It's not a sappy romance or a cookie cutter story. It follows Siobhán and Annie through a bit of a whirlwind, but yet believable courtship and well into the building of their relationship. Their personalities ring true as do their experiences within their own lives. It's not all hearts and flowers either but there's a balance to it all that makes it work. I definitely recommend this story and author."

-Becky Gard

A Brighter Palette

Palette

by
Brigham Vaughn

This is a work of fiction. Names, characters, businesses, places, events and incidents are either the products of the author's imagination or used in a fictitious manner. Any resemblance to actual persons, living or dead, or actual events is purely coincidental.

© Brigham Vaughn
ISBN-13: 978-1979620895
ISBN: 197962089X

Cover design by Brigham Vaughn
Book design and production by Brigham Vaughn
Editing by Sally Hopkinson
Cover Images: © sasamihajlovic/Adobe Stock
© sasamihajlovic/Adobe Stock

Printed in the United States of America

First Printing, 2017

Published by Two Peninsulas Press

TWO PENINSULAS PRESS

Acknowledgements

This story was inspired by a flash fiction I did on my blog almost two years ago. I've been wanting to tell Annie and Siobhán's story ever since.

Other than major city landmarks, most of the destinations mentioned in *A Brighter Palette* are fictitious or loosely based on an amalgam of real places. I describe Annie as having worked for "The Boston Chronicle". Although there is no current newspaper in Boston with that name, it *was* a colonial paper published from 1767-1770. I thought the name would be a nice nod to Annie's love of early American history. Siobhán's style of painting isn't based on any one artist in particular, but I did enjoy researching current lesbian art and I'd highly recommend taking the time to search for it. There are some beautiful pieces available.

I want to thank Chris K. who helped me create Annie's journalism background. Thanks for putting up with me pestering you with questions about whether or not Annie's career history was plausible. I appreciate your help so much! I also want to thank my beta readers for their help on the story. Allison, K. Evan, and Helena provided much-needed feedback and I appreciate their hard work so much. In particular, K. Evan helped with the Boston fact-checking, and Helena helped with the Irish side of things. The story wouldn't be the same without them. Huge thanks to Sally Hopkinson for her fast, accurate, editing work. I couldn't do this without you!

As always, big thanks to the bloggers and readers who love my work and spread the news about it. Your reviews and mentions on social media help immensely. And welcome to any new readers. I hope you enjoy Annie and Siobhán's story.

Table of Contents

Chapter One
June

"**P**retentious twat, isn't he?" The words were harsh, but the lilt of an Irish accent softened them.

Annie Slocum glanced over her shoulder to see a slim, dark-haired woman smiling at her. Annie pressed her hand to her chest as if that would somehow slow her suddenly racing heart. She wasn't sure if it was because she hadn't noticed someone standing behind her or because the person in question was so stunning.

She wore a fitted black dress that hugged her subtle curves, and the long sweep of her hair was nearly as dark as the fabric she wore, a beautiful contrast to her creamy skin. Annie was so absorbed in the lilt of her accent and her beauty that it took her a moment to put the pieces together. The words finally registered, and Annie figured out who on earth she was calling a pretentious twat.

"Who? Uh, Gabriel?" Annie asked, clearing her throat and hoping the other woman hadn't noticed her too-long pause. Gabriel Quinn, the gallery owner, had been droning on about the color and composition of a nearby piece the entire time Annie had been standing there. All while wearing a vintage-looking suit and fedora. On top of his habit of being an insufferable bore, it was a good bet that was whom the woman was talking about.

She nodded. "Yes. Gabriel likes to hear himself talk. He sells my paintings, so I can't complain much, but he's always goin' on about the deeper meaning where there is none."

Stunned, Annie turned to face her fully. "You're Siobhán Murray."

The Quinn Gallery in the Charlestown area of Boston had put together a show of local, female artists. Annie had begun to think the night was a wash

1

until Siobhán's work caught her eye. She'd spent a while lingering over her paintings.

"I am." A smile quirked up the corners of her lush mouth. "I'm impressed that you pronounced it correctly."

Siobhán was a challenge for American tongues, but the lilting of an Irish voice saying *Shi-vonne* sounded so beautiful.

"Oh, I spent a semester in Dublin in college," Annie explained. "I met several Siobháns there."

"Well, that explains it." They exchanged smiles.

"Ann Slocum." She held out her hand. "Or Annie, if you prefer."

"Annie." Her name rolled off Siobhán's tongue in a way that sent a shiver up her spine. "And a Slocum at that. English heritage?"

"Yes. Hopefully, you won't hold that against me."

Siobhán laughed. "I try not to let national rivalries get in the way of talking with a beautiful woman. Well, except for rugby. You don't root for the English rugby team, do you?"

"I don't root for anyone. I don't watch any sports at all unless I'm forced to," Annie explained with a smile. She was starting to think she and Siobhán might bat for the same team, however. The compliment and heady eye contact hadn't gone unnoticed.

Siobhán stepped closer. "So what brings you to my showing?"

"Oh, I got an invitation from Gabriel. He knows I like art and try to support local female artists."

Siobhán tilted her head. "You know Gabriel personally then?"

"We go way back." Annie's laugh was a touch uncomfortable. She never really knew how to explain her relationship with Gabriel.

An odd expression crossed Siobhán's face. "Perhaps I shouldn't have run my mouth off then."

Chuckling, Annie waved off Siobhán's concern. "Oh, I'm certainly not about to go tattling to him about what you said. It isn't my style, and we aren't that close. We went to school together, and he dated my roommate at the time. Gabriel and I stayed acquaintances. He's a nice enough guy, just pretentious."

"We're in agreement about Gabriel then." Her laugh was throaty, and the timbre sent a tingle through Annie. Damn. It had been a long time since she'd found a woman this attractive. Siobhán tilted her head toward the canvas Annie had been examining. "What do you think of it?"

"I love it," Annie answered honestly, turning to look at the piece again. It was a painting of a woman in profile with rainbow washes of color and an intriguing crackle technique. Now that she'd met the artist, Annie realized it was a self-portrait.

Siobhán's upper arm pressed against hers as they stood there in silence for a moment. Annie suppressed a shudder at the contact. Summers in Boston were usually quite warm, and Siobhán's dress and Annie's shirt were both sleeveless. Siobhán's bare skin was soft and cool from the over-air-conditioned gallery.

"In the market for art?" Siobhán's tone was light, but it occurred to Annie that the attention could be because Siobhán was hoping to sell her work. Perhaps the flirtatious looks had been nothing but a sales tactic. The thought left Annie feeling strangely deflated, but she plastered a smile on her face and answered honestly.

"I'm afraid not. Your work is worth far more than a journalist's salary would allow."

"Oh! You aren't here to critique the show, are you?"

"No. I'm not an art critic. I do freelance work for various sites. Mostly fluff pieces. It's a far cry from the investigative reporting I studied in college, but it pays the bills." *More or less*, Annie thought. "My interest in art is entirely amateur."

"I'd love to hear more about what you think of it. No pressure, but I'm quite curious." If Siobhán had been flirting with Annie to make a sale or get a good review, learning that Annie would be no use to her would have been her cue to leave, but to Annie's surprise and pleasure, she didn't seem to be going anywhere.

Annie studied the painting for a few moments. "At first glance, it seems vibrant, but the colors are actually rather subdued. Deep, but not bright. She,

3

well, *you*"—Annie corrected—"seems contemplative. Not sad, exactly, but like you're lost in thought."

"You have a good eye," Siobhán said with a smile.

"The crackle technique is interesting too," Annie commented. "I'm curious though; does it have a deeper meaning?"

"Not particularly; I was just experimenting with new ideas. It doesn't represent 'my crumbling self-esteem' like Gabriel suggested when I first showed the piece to him."

"No wonder you called him a pretentious twat," Annie murmured. They exchanged wry grins. "So that little smudge of red there"—Annie traced her finger in the air over the spot on the painting—"doesn't have deeper meaning either?"

Siobhán snorted delicately. "Hardly. I probably just needed to add a bit of color for contrast or balance and happened to have red on my brush at the time."

Annie's laugh was genuine. She loved art—always had—but she'd met a few too many artists in her life to believe all the pompous bullshit some of them spouted. She'd found that the ones who spoke the most about their own art had the least to say about anything else in life.

"Would you like to grab a drink?" Siobhán laid a hand on Annie's arm. She had to suppress another shiver. "I'd like to talk to you more."

"Here?" Annie glanced around the bright, contemporary space. There were wait staff wandering the gallery with drinks and appetizers, but it wasn't ideal for having a conversation.

"There's a hotel next door." Annie's surprise must have shown on her face because Siobhán's smile widened. "With an excellent restaurant and bar. Have you eaten? I haven't had a thing since lunch."

"I had a light dinner a few hours ago," Annie admitted. "But I could have another bite. Should you leave your show before it's over though?"

"Probably not." Siobhán sighed. "I'm trying to decide how much I care right now."

Annie glanced at the slim gold watch on her wrist. "It's supposed to wrap up at nine, isn't it?"

"Yes."

"That's less than half an hour. Why don't you finish up here? I'll take a final look around the gallery while you wait," Annie offered.

"You don't mind?" Siobhán's glance was searching.

"Not at all."

"If you finish before I'm done, you can always head over to the lounge. I can meet you there."

"I'm looking forward to it," Annie said, catching Siobhán's gaze.

"I am too," she said huskily. "Very much."

It was nearly nine-thirty when Siobhán flew into the hotel lounge, breathless and apologetic. "I am terribly sorry, Annie. I'm so relieved to see you're still here. I was afraid you'd left."

Annie had been less than five minutes from paying her tab and leaving. She smiled at Siobhán. "I was contemplating it, but I'm glad I stayed."

Siobhán unwound a crimson scarf from around her throat and dropped it and a black leather purse onto the far side of the circular booth before sliding in next to Annie.

"I'd love to blame it on Gabriel."

Annie chuckled. "Is he to blame?"

Siobhán's blue eyes sparkled. "He is, but it was for a good cause. He introduced me to a couple interested in commissioning a piece. I rarely work on commission, but this sounds very intriguing. I may pursue it. I hope you'll forgive me. I hated to keep you waiting."

Annie smiled at her. "I can hardly complain about an artist making a potential sale at her own gallery show."

Siobhán waved off her comment, her amber bracelet sliding down her slim forearm. "Still, me ma raised me better than that. I'm glad you stayed. It occurred to me I didn't have your mobile number to let you know I was running late."

5

"Is that your subtle way of asking for my number?" There was a flirtatious note to Annie's voice that she hardly recognized. God, she'd been in a rut lately. She'd forgotten how much fun flirting was.

Siobhán propped her left elbow on the table, put her chin on her hand, and leaned in. "Haven't I already made it clear how interested I am?" She skimmed the fingertips of her right hand along Annie's forearm.

The touch raised gooseflesh on Annie's arms, and she again suppressed a shiver. "I wanted to be sure."

Siobhán leaned even closer, her lips barely brushing the shell of Annie's ear. "If I haven't made it crystal clear, I am very interested in you, Annie Slocum." She continued stroking Annie's arm, her fingertips tracing little patterns as she moved toward the inside of Annie's wrist. Hyperaware of Siobhán's touch, she let her eyes drift shut. She held her breath as Siobhán's thumb rubbed the sensitive spot. "I want to get to know you. Every single bit of you."

Someone delicately cleared their throat, and Annie's eyes flew open to see the waitress standing near the table. "Is there anything I can get you? Another white wine, ma'am?"

"Oh, uh." Annie glanced at her empty wineglass, flustered. "Yes, please."

"And for you?" She looked at Siobhán.

"Coffee, please. With a shot of Tullamore Dew if you have it, please. Bushmills Black, if you don't."

"We do carry the Tullamore. An appetizer or a dessert to go along with it perhaps?"

Annie shook her head.

"I'll just nibble on what's here if Annie doesn't mind," Siobhán said.

"No, no, of course not." Annie wondered if the innuendo had been intentional. "I got it for both of us." Truthfully, she'd been so nervous about Siobhán arriving, she'd barely managed a few bites of the cheese plate she'd ordered.

"I'll be back shortly with your drinks then." The waitress disappeared.

6

Although Siobhán hadn't removed her hand from Annie's wrist while the waitress was there, she let go now and reached for a cracker. "I hope I haven't made you uncomfortable."

Annie shook her head. "I don't usually lose track of my surroundings so thoroughly," she admitted. "But I'm not sorry I did."

Siobhán brushed her fingertips against Annie's honey-blonde hair where it draped across her shoulder. "You're out then?"

Annie laughed. "Oh, I came out as bi in college. Which is longer ago than I like to admit."

Siobhán's mouth turned down at the corners as she frowned. "You're bisexual?"

"Yes." Annie raised an eyebrow. "Is that a problem?"

Siobhán hesitated. "I've had a few less than great experiences with bi women, unfortunately."

"And I've had a few less than great experiences with lesbian women who look down on me for being bi," Annie said calmly. Her heart sank. How many times was she going to have to go through this? How many times would she think things were going great with a woman, only to have her hopes dashed when the truth came out?

The furrow on Siobhán's brow smoothed out. "I suppose we all have our baggage, don't we?" Her tone was light, and she resumed toying with the ends of Annie's hair.

"I suppose we do." Annie smiled at her. Well, maybe her identity was a minor bump in the road instead of a full barrier. She could live with that. She shifted in her seat to look Siobhán in the eye. God, she was beautiful.

"You're a journalist, you said?"

"Yes, but mostly freelance these days," Annie said ruefully. "The newspaper business isn't exactly booming. Most of the bigger papers are cutting back. And truthfully, by the time I got out of college, I was pretty disillusioned with the field. Freelance work can be very hit or miss. Sometimes I enjoy the topic I'm writing about. Sometimes I don't. It's feast or famine with my income. I love the flexibility of my schedule but there are certainly no traditional benefits like health insurance or a retirement plan."

Siobhán made a face and reached for a chunk of cheese. "There's a lot to be said for this country, but you have a strange obsession with self-sufficiency. Even to your own detriment."

"Tell me about it," Annie agreed. She opened her mouth to continue, but the waitress appeared with their drinks.

"Please, excuse the delay. The coffee was old, so I had them brew a fresh pot."

Siobhán smiled at her. "Thanks, love."

Annie received her wine with a smile and thank you, but once the waitress was gone, she turned back to Siobhán. "So, tell me more about your art. I'm fascinated."

"What would you like to know?"

"How did you get started?"

"Oh, growing up, I was always scribbling on something or other," Siobhán said with a smile. "Me ma moved the bed once to find I'd been doodling on the walls. She made me repaint it, but I just started over again, and she finally gave up and let me do a mural on one wall."

Annie smiled at the thought. "Were you a bit of a hellion?"

"I might have been." Siobhán's teeth flashed white as she smiled. "I used to sneak out of the house often. Then, when I got older, I'd sneak girls in."

"Corrupting the local girls, huh?"

"Like you wouldn't believe." There was a soft purring edge to Siobhán's voice that made Annie shift in her seat. "I was the cause of half the girls in our parish confessing to the priest about their lesbian sins."

"I think I would have liked teenage Siobhán," Annie teased. She took another sip of her wine.

"Teenage Siobhán would have enjoyed you as well." She peered at Annie over the rim of her glass mug. The scent of whiskey and coffee filled the air. "The question is, were you one of the naïve, innocent ones or the secretly wanton ones?"

"Neither," Annie said with a rueful laugh. "I was the oblivious one. I used to fool around with the neighbor girl, but I had no idea what I was doing or that all girls didn't do it together."

Siobhán smiled and smeared a bit of goat cheese on a piece of baguette. "I still remember the first time I rubbed up against another girl. We can't have been more than twelve, but I thought we had invented the act."

"I think first sex is always like that." Annie shifted again, aware of the growing tension inside her.

Siobhán licked a smear of goat cheese from her thumb and dropped her hand to Annie's thigh. "I think good sex should always feel like that." Her voice held a hint of husky promise. "If you're doing it right, it will, anyway."

Annie took another gulp of her wine. She felt strangely nervous around Siobhán. Her sexuality was so on the surface. She didn't seem to hide behind all of the false modesty like so many women—Annie included—did. Instead, it seemed to seep from her every pore and drip from her lush mouth.

"I can't remember the last time it felt that way for me," Annie admitted. "With a man or a woman. It's so easy to fall into that rut where it's satisfying but not passionate."

Siobhán gently stroked her thigh through the soft fabric. "Oh, but passion is the best part. That breathless sense of anticipation and need where you can't even think straight because you want the other person so much." Her hand crept higher on Annie's leg, moving toward her inner thigh. "Don't you agree, Annie?"

"I'm very quickly becoming re-acquainted with it," Annie admitted. Her fingers tightened on the stem of the wineglass as if it would somehow anchor her.

Without conscious thought, Annie parted her thighs, allowing Siobhán's slender fingers to slip between. Annie felt a sudden rush of regret that she hadn't worn a skirt as Siobhán teased the seam of her trousers, gently pushing it between her lips. She could feel the silky fabric of her panties dampening and clinging to her aroused skin. The slight ache of desire grew, and she shifted, pressing into the teasing, probing touch. Siobhán's finger grazed her clit, and even through two layers of fabric, it sent a delicious wave of pleasure through her.

"Oh," she said, the words flowing out of her on a sigh.

9

"Careful, love," Siobhán murmured in her ear, her lips brushing the shell and making another shudder run straight through Annie. "As much as I'm enjoying your reactions, we wouldn't want to let everyone else know how well this date is going."

The words brought Annie up short as she was reminded of where they were. Flushing, she straightened and closed her legs. Siobhán's hand was trapped between, and she gave Annie a wicked smile. She wiggled her hand free—sending another jolt of pleasure through Annie—and squeezed her thigh. "Forgot where we were?"

"I did. I'm so embarrassed." Annie pressed her palms to her cheeks. "I got a little carried away."

Siobhán straightened but didn't slide away. "I enjoyed watching you get carried away. We'll have to do that again when we aren't in such a public place."

Annie glanced around. Thankfully, the lighting was subdued. They were toward the back of the nearly empty lounge, and the backs of the booths had dividers. Unless a waitress had walked by, it was unlikely anyone had seen them.

"This is so unlike me," Annie admitted.

Siobhán tilted her chin and gave Annie an appraising look. "Perhaps it's just what you need."

Annie's embarrassment began to fade, and she offered Siobhán a small smile. "I certainly could use a bit more excitement in my life," she admitted. "Although, that doesn't necessarily include a public exhibition."

"Public exhibition is optional," Siobhán said, "but passion shouldn't be."

Chapter Two

Annie's pulse beat strongly as she exited the cab and waited for Siobhán to follow suit. They stood in front of an older, brick row house in Charlestown, just on the other side of the Charles River from North Boston.

Siobhán captured her fingers and gently tugged her toward the front door. Annie wanted to make small talk or comment on what a beautiful building it was, but the thought that they were headed straight for Siobhán's place left her mute.

She'd been so eager she hadn't thought twice when Siobhán had asked her if she wanted to come back to her place. But the cab ride there had allowed her far too much time to think, even with the distracting feel of Siobhán's blunt nails tracing up and down her thigh and the occasional murmured promise in her ear.

God, it had been months since she'd slept with a woman—or a man for that matter—and it just occurred to her that she hadn't tidied up her bikini line recently. She'd gone to the gallery expecting to admire art, not end up in bed with an artist, so although her underarms and legs were smooth, her bush was a little wild. She cringed at the thought.

As they reached the landing of the stairs, her nerves went haywire, and she felt a sudden, clutching moment of panic, wondering if she should just make up an excuse and beg to reschedule.

"You're thinking too much," Siobhán murmured, pressing her up against the old, wooden railing. She kissed Annie before she could reply. "Just relax. Let go, love."

Siobhán pulled back and tugged her up the second set of stairs. Annie was too dazed and turned on by the kiss to argue. Siobhán let her into the apartment, immediately dumping her scarf and handbag on the couch. She kicked off her heels, and Annie had a brief glimpse of a charming little living room before she heard the distinctive sound of a zipper.

11

Siobhán stood with her arms behind her as she pulled the zipper down. She let out a seductive little wiggle, and Annie gulped when the black dress hit the wood floor.

Clad in nothing but a pretty black lace bra and panties, Siobhán spun on her heel and disappeared down the hall. "I'll be in the bedroom," she called over her shoulder, and her words finally spurred Annie into action. As she followed, she caught a glimpse of the bra on the hallway floor and then a lace-clad ass disappeared through a door.

She must live alone, Annie thought wildly as she quickened her pace.

She entered the bedroom in time to see Siobhán step out of her panties, illuminated by the single lamp beside the bed. God, she was perfect. Her body was slender but more softly rounded than Annie's angular frame. Her waist was narrow, and her hips flared out into gentle curves that made Annie's mouth water.

Siobhán stretched out on the white sheets, and Annie couldn't tear her eyes away from her breasts. They were high and firm, the nipples darkly rosy. C-cup at least, and Annie wanted to bury her face between them. A wave of shyness swept over her, and she stood at the side of the bed, frozen.

"Aren't you going to join me?"

Annie nodded mutely and reached for the hem of her shirt. Her pulse pounded in her ears, and her fingers felt clumsy and uncoordinated. She dropped the shirt to the ground, followed by her trousers, then looked over at the bed. Her breasts were smaller than Siobhán's and her hips narrower. *Am I too bony?* she wondered.

Siobhán sat up gracefully, propping herself on one elbow to watch Annie. The look on Siobhán's face was hungry, and it gave Annie the courage to continue. With clumsy fingers, Annie unhooked her bra and dropped it on top of her clothes. She hooked her fingers on the edge of her panties and pushed them down before she could second-guess herself.

"I can hear your mind going like an out of control train," Siobhán said softly, beckoning to Annie. "But I have no idea why. You're lovely. Come here and let me show you how much I want you."

The words gave Annie the courage to step forward and kneel on the bed. Siobhán reached for her, drawing her close. Siobhán's skin felt cool against Annie's, and she gasped quietly when they were pressed together full-length. Siobhán kissed her, re-igniting the simmering heat that had been banked by

12

nerves. Annie shuddered and returned the kiss with equal fervor. Siobhán rolled her onto her back and kissed her way down Annie's chin to her neck.

She peppered kisses and small nips of her teeth down Annie's chest, stopping to circle one nipple, then the other with a warm, wet tongue. Annie gasped, feeling the throb in her clit as Siobhán sucked. She alternated between Annie's breasts, sucking, licking, and nibbling until Annie writhed under her.

"Please," Annie begged, feeling breathless and desperate. She gripped the sheets below her as Siobhán moved lower, kissing her midriff and down to her hip. Annie felt the brush of soft hair against her inner thigh as Siobhán pressed her legs apart and traced her tongue along the crest of Annie's hipbone.

She cried out but Siobhán merely tongued her way over to Annie's other hip, as if she had all the time in the world. Annie felt like sobbing when she moved lower, nipping and kissing her inner thighs but ignoring what lay between them. Annie had a vague, embarrassed thought that she was probably already dripping onto the sheets below her, but the warm, gentle lap of a tongue on her pussy sent her head spinning.

She reached down, gathering Siobhán's hair in her hands as she tried to wordlessly encourage her to continue. But Siobhán seemed to need no encouragement as she traced her tongue up and down Annie's lips before teasing between them. Siobhán made a low, satisfied sound in the back of her throat before she pushed Annie's thighs up and back and swiped the flat of her tongue against Annie's lips, grazing across her clit.

Annie closed her eyes and gave in to the feel of Siobhán's clever mouth and wet, probing tongue. Siobhán licked her with gusto, like she was devouring a delicious meal she couldn't get enough of. Annie panted with pleasure as Siobhán licked and sucked at her clit, drawing her close to the edge, then easing back, over and over, until Annie writhed on the bed and whimpered, lost and uninhibited in her pleasure. When Siobhán found a particularly sensitive spot, Annie's grip tightened on her head.

"There, yeah, right there," Annie quietly pleaded.

Siobhán used her thumbs to open Annie up farther and flicked her tongue across Annie's clit more firmly. She didn't let up when Annie threw her head back and cried out. The muscles in her inner thighs twitched as the orgasm went on and on. Siobhán didn't stop until Annie was so over-sensitive she had to weakly push Siobhán away. She rested her head on Annie's stomach

13

and ran her fingers up and down Annie's thighs, sending little aftershocks of ticklish pleasure through her as she slowly came down from the mind-blowing pleasure.

Eventually, Siobhán slid up the bed and pressed a kiss to her shoulder. Annie felt wrung out and boneless, but she reached for Siobhán and managed to grab her hand. "Oh my God, that was ..."

Siobhán propped herself up on one elbow and smiled at her. "For me too, love."

"I can't remember the last time I came like that." It occurred to Annie that she'd left Siobhán hanging. "But you ... I should ..."

Siobhán silenced her with a languid kiss. "We'll get there. I've got all night, unless you're going somewhere?"

Annie laughed and reached up to push Siobhán's dark hair away from her face. "God, no. I don't want to move from this bed."

Possibly ever, she added in her head and kissed Siobhán, tasting herself on her lover's lips.

"**H**ow long have you been in the U.S.?" Annie asked a while later. She and Siobhán sat on the bed as they finished a bowl of grapes and a few bites of rich, dark chocolate. It felt incredibly decadent. Annie had covered her lower half with the sheet while they ate but Siobhán lounged against the headboard naked. She had, in fact, prepared their snack naked, as well, while Annie lay in her bed and tried not to wonder about what happened next.

"Twelve ... thirteen years?" Siobhán reached for the glass of wine on the nightstand. "I'd finished university in Dublin and decided I wanted to see more of the world. My grandmother lived here, and I still have a couple cousins in Boston, so it was a natural choice."

She swallowed a mouthful of the wine, then handed the glass to Annie, who drained the small remainder.

"You didn't have any trouble getting a green card?" Annie asked, curious. She waved off the plate Siobhán held out to her. "A lesbian couple I know had a massive struggle."

14

Siobhán moved the remainder of their snack off the bed and stretched out on her stomach. "I have dual citizenship. Da's Irish and me ma was American."

Annie set the now-empty glass on the other nightstand, then settled on her side. She stroked her fingers up and down Siobhán's bare back. "God, that accent of yours."

To her surprise, Siobhán flushed. "Impenetrable, isn't it?"

"No, sexy," Annie said. She leaned in to kiss Siobhán's shoulder. "Very, very sexy."

"You must have enjoyed yourself in Ireland then," Siobhán murmured.

"I did." Annie smiled, remembering the redheaded woman she'd shared a bed with for most of the semester.

Siobhán's grin was salacious. "That sounds like a story I'd like to hear."

"Really?" Annie asked with a laugh. "You want to hear about Brigid, the pretty redhead I dated? Or about the time her roommate almost caught us? I had my head between her legs when the poor girl walked in the room."

"How naughty. I love that. You're so cool and collected on the outside, Annie, but once we started talking, I could see the passionate side eager to get out."

"I used to have a very passionate side," Annie admitted. "Actually, what I told you about the redhead wasn't the whole story. There's a lot more to it."

"I'm intrigued." Siobhán propped her chin up on her hand.

"Well, Nora—her roommate—was definitely shocked. But she was less horrified than Brigid and I expected." Annie felt her cheeks heat a little. "One night a week or so later, the three of us had a few drinks, and well, Nora confessed she was curious."

Siobhán raised an eyebrow. "Curious about women?"

"Yes."

"Go on then."

Annie laughed. "Well, one thing led to another, and it wasn't long before I was in bed with two women. And Brigid and I showed Nora just how good it could be."

"Mmm, you little minx. And what did she think in the morning?"

"Oh, we'd thoroughly converted her to our ways," Annie said with a laugh. "I don't think she had another date with a guy for the rest of the semester."

"And did she find her way into another threesome with you and Brigid?"

"A few times," Annie admitted. "In fact, after my going-away party, I staggered back to their room and had one hell of a going-away after-party." She grinned at Siobhán. "And then I felt like I was going to die on the flight home to Boston."

"Worth it though?"

"Totally." Annie sighed. "But after I got back to the U.S., I threw myself into school and work, and everything else fell by the wayside. I felt like I had to grow up and be serious. Focus on my career, find the right partner, make the smart choices. Until tonight, it had been a very long time since my passionate side had come out."

"Why were you keeping her locked away?"

Annie rolled onto her back and stared at the ceiling. "Fear, I suppose. After my last relationship went south, I just couldn't work up the courage to try again." She sighed. "So, my love life was boring, my job was boring, and I felt boring. Boring leads to more boring. I was just waiting for something to come along and wake me up."

Siobhán sat up and straddled Annie, her dark hair falling like a curtain around them. "Well, here I am."

She leaned down and kissed Annie, her mouth tasting of wine and chocolate now.

Here you are, Annie thought, and she wasn't sure if it was nerves or excitement that coursed through her when she realized she had no idea if this was one night or the promise of something more.

Siobhán was still sleeping when Annie awoke. She lay on her stomach, sheet and blanket twisted around her hips, leaving her legs and back bare. The air was still and quiet, and sunlight peeked in through the curtains, striping Siobhán's body with light. Annie was no artist, but she wished she could capture the quiet stillness of the moment.

Instead, she slipped out of bed and padded quietly to the bathroom down the hall. A small, potted fern hung from a hook near the window, and the creamy yellow vintage tiles were accented with little splashes of color from the towels and rug. A few framed art pieces were hung on the walls, but none of them looked like Siobhán's work.

Annie groaned when she caught sight of herself in the antique mirror over the sink. She was a complete and utter mess. Her makeup was smeared around her eyes and worn off elsewhere, and her hair looked like birds had been nesting in it. She tidied up the best she could with what she had stashed in her purse and returned to the bedroom.

She hadn't paid much attention to the bedroom the night before, but it was charming. Siobhán's bed was situated along the wall across from the door, and a single window filled the adjacent one. The room felt warm and welcoming, from the scarred wooden floors partially covered by the soft wool rug to the wrought iron headboard.

A vintage wooden dresser sat next to the door. A few pieces of jewelry were scattered across the top, like she'd dressed hastily before she left for the gallery and hadn't had time to tidy up since.

Reluctantly, Annie reached for her clothes. They were draped over a small upholstered bench at the foot of the bed where Siobhán had left them the night before when she got up to make them the snack.

Annie pulled on her clothes and had just finished dressing when Siobhán stirred. She turned onto her back, then frowned at Annie.

"Leaving without saying goodbye?" Siobhán's voice was husky. They'd left the curtains partially open and a stripe of sunlight illuminated her breasts and gave her face a warm glow. Her hair was dark against the white pillowcase. The duvet was white too, with bright streaks of color from flowers that looked almost hand-painted. She was so beautiful it hurt to look at her. Like a woman painted by Titian or Botticelli in a sea of impressionist flowers.

Annie gestured to the nightstand. "I left a note. I didn't want to wake you, but I did tell you I hoped to see you again and left my number."

Siobhán dragged a hand through her hair, then wiped under her eyes where her eyeliner was smudged. "Ugh. I must look a mess."

Annie stared at her for a long moment, then shook her head. "You look beautiful. God, I don't want to leave," she blurted out.

"So don't." Siobhán gracefully shifted so she was on her hands and knees. She crawled toward Annie, her gaze never leaving Annie's face. "Stay in bed with me."

Annie laughed faintly. "All day?"

Siobhán straightened until she was kneeling on the bed and slid warm hands under Annie's blouse. She leaned in and nibbled Annie's neck. "All day. All night. Until we're starving and have to venture out. Until I've given you so many orgasms you're too weak for another. Until we've had our fill."

"What if I have somewhere to be?" Annie said weakly, but she tangled her hands in Siobhán's thick hair and guided her mouth to the spot that always made her knees go wobbly.

"Do you?" Siobhán flicked her tongue against it, and sure enough, Annie's knees sagged. Siobhán used the opportunity to pull Annie down onto the white sheets. She went willingly.

"Do I what?" Annie gasped. Siobhán had made short work of her blouse and somehow her bra was unhooked, and then, *oh God*, her warm hands toyed with Annie's nipples.

"Have somewhere to be?"

Siobhán looked her in the eye, and Annie thought of the errands she should run and the blog post that was due and the laundry piling up. The only words that came out of her mouth were, "Here. In your bed."

Siobhán grinned and reached for the waistband of her pants, but Annie shook her head and slid down Siobhán's naked body. Throughout the night, they'd gone down on each other too many times to keep track of, but Annie was dying to feel the soft, wet flesh under her tongue again.

Siobhán let her knees fall open and Annie took a moment to appreciate the gorgeous view in front of her. Siobhán had the most beautiful pussy Annie had ever seen, pinky-brown with folds that invited Annie to explore deeper. Annie kissed the soft patch of hair above, then licked her way down

Siobhán's smooth lips. They were plump and full, parting to reveal darker inner lips that always seemed to be slick with moisture.

The sweet, musky scent of her pulled Annie in to taste, and she gently slipped a finger inside. Siobhán moaned, her thighs tensing against Annie's ears as Annie began to move, the soft, wet flesh enveloping her thrusting finger. She hadn't been sure if Siobhán would like it. Not all women did, and some lesbians were especially put off by any kind of penetration, but Siobhán seemed to enjoy it. Her fingers tangled in Annie's hair, pulling her in and directing her mouth to her clit.

"Oh, yes," Siobhán moaned. "Oh, *Annie.*"

Annie traced firm circles around the pearl of her clit, feeling the little jolts of pleasure that went through Siobhán's body when she hit just the right spot. Annie worshipped Siobhán with her tongue and fingers, coaxing her through several orgasms until her skin glistened with sweat and she trembled underneath her.

"Annie." Siobhán murmured something Annie couldn't translate in soft, lilting Irish and drew her up so they lay tangled together on the bed, their heads resting on the same pillow. "*Mo álainn.*"

Annie had known what that meant at some point, but for the life of her, she couldn't think of what it was.

Annie cupped Siobhán's cheek and stared into her blue eyes. It felt like she was drowning, tumbling head over heels, and yet she'd never felt more clear or sure that this was exactly what her life had been missing.

Chapter Three

Annie awoke sometime late in the morning and reached out for Siobhán, only to find herself alone in the bed. She burrowed under the covers for a moment, feeling content and happy for the first time in months. She flipped onto her back and stretched, feeling the pull of long-neglected muscles in her thighs and abs that ached from the orgasms. It put a smile on her face.

The air smelled of coffee, and Annie ventured out of bed to investigate.

She found a T-shirt folded on the nightstand that hadn't been there before, so she slipped it on. Although clearly freshly laundered, Siobhán's scent still seemed to cling to it, sweet like milk and honey, and warm like fresh baked bread. With a womanly, earthy undertone that made Annie want to bury her face between Siobhán's thighs and never leave. Annie smoothed the thin, soft fabric over her body and glanced at herself in the mirror hanging from the closet door. Her legs were thin, but long, and strong from the running she did. In Siobhán's shirt, she felt sexy. Or maybe it was the hours of orgasms that brightened her normally pale cheeks and gave her that soft, contented smile.

The bathroom was empty, although there was a toothbrush—still in the package—on the corner of the little pedestal sink. Annie brushed her teeth with the toothpaste she found on the nearby shelf crammed full of beauty products.

When her teeth were clean and her mouth no longer tasted like sleep, Annie finger combed through her shoulder-length blonde hair, wiped away a stray smear of mascara from under her eyes, and gave herself another critical glance. "It'll have to do," she muttered.

She followed the scent of paint down the hall and found Siobhán in the small, sunlit living room. Although maybe art studio with a couch was a better word. One wall was mostly taken up by windows. Plastic drop cloths were set up underneath them and an easel, stool, and table took up most of the space. The couch—loveseat really—was crammed in a corner opposite a small television on an antique-looking wooden dresser. A fabric ottoman, covered with newspapers and books, sat between.

Everything was done in warm, neutral tones with little splashes of color from the tumble of pillows on the loveseat and the canvases on the walls. The look was slightly Bohemian but sophisticated.

Siobhán stood with her back to Annie, painting. She wore a loose, gray tank top that had slipped down one shoulder and her black hair was twisted up in a messy bun, held in place by what looked like a paintbrush. Annie watched her for a few moments, enjoying the sight of the smooth, firm strokes that left a trail of red paint in its wake.

"Are you going to gawp all day or come give me a kiss, love?" Siobhán teased, her back still to Annie.

She felt an odd jolt, like a sense of déjà vu. Or a premonition of what it would be like to be Siobhán's partner. To wake up every morning and see this. The moment was new, yet somehow familiar, and it left Annie with a funny feeling in the center of her chest.

She crossed the room to Siobhán, who craned her neck and offered her lips to Annie. Perched on the stool, she sat a little lower than Annie, who had to lean down to kiss her. Siobhán tasted of coffee, and when she drew back, she smiled up at her.

"I see you found the shirt and the toothbrush I left."

"I did," Annie said with a smile. "Thank you. That was thoughtful."

She refrained from asking if Siobhán had so many overnight guests it was routine, or if that had been just for her. She wasn't sure she wanted to know. A woman like Siobhán would have no trouble finding lovers.

"I'd offer to make you coffee or tea but I'm afraid I'm covered in paint," Siobhán said apologetically. "You'll have to either make it yourself or give me a few minutes to finish and clean up."

"I've got it," Annie said. "Just point me in the direction of your kitchen and tell me what kind of coffee maker you have."

"Through the French doors there, and the cafetière is on the counter. I'm afraid you'll have to clean the pot before you make yours," Siobhán said.

21

"The ground coffee and the sugar should be on the counter though, and cream is in the refrigerator."

"Thanks. I'm sure I can handle it." Annie smiled and pressed a kiss to Siobhán's cheek.

She stepped through half-open French doors into the tiny kitchen. A small bistro table and two chairs took up the spot under the window. Plants hung in front of the window and dotted the sill in between colored glass bottles and fancy tea tins.

Annie found the coffee press on the counter beside the sink and a tray with all the necessary ingredients near it. She located the trashcan below the sink, scraped the used grounds into it, and then rinsed the pot. She hummed tunelessly to herself as she filled a kettle with water and turned the burner on to heat it, then poured the coffee into the press.

While she waited for the water to heat, she looked around the room. The kitchen was barely large enough to turn around in, but it was charming. Red, turquoise, and green Fiestaware dishes lined the open-shelves above the small stove and a red dishtowel was looped around the handle of the refrigerator.

From what she'd seen, the entire apartment was old but bright and clean. The clutter seemed homey, and when Annie mentally compared it to her own cramped apartment that she shared with three roommates, she frowned. She hardly ventured out of her own bedroom when she was at home, and although the kitchen was an ample size, she was always disgusted by the dishes that were left on the counters and in the sink. Half the time, she didn't even want to be at home. When she could afford to, she took her laptop to a nearby coffee shop to work just so she could get out of the house and away from her roommates.

Annie peered at the photos scattered across the fridge and smiled at the sight of Siobhán on a beach with a pail full of clams next to her and a broad grin on her face. There was also one of her with an older couple. Siobhán wore a thick, white sweater and looked barely out of her teens. Given the green fields behind them, Annie would guess it was from when she was still living in Ireland. And from the couple's resemblance to Siobhán, it was probably a picture with her parents. Annie could see the shape of Siobhán's eyes in her father's face, but the rest of her seemed to have come from her extraordinarily beautiful mother.

The whistle of the teakettle pulled her away, and she clicked off the gas. Unable to find a potholder, she used the dishtowel to pour the water into the pot to brew. "Do you want some coffee, Siobhán?" she called out as she retrieved a turquoise mug from the hook on the wall.

"Not right now, thanks, Annie!"

"Want me to make breakfast?"

"Oh, sure. That would be grand."

Annie smiled and stirred the coffee before putting the lid on and allowing it to steep for a few more minutes. She found eggs, butter, and chives in the refrigerator and a partial loaf of bread on top of it.

She was sipping coffee and scrambling eggs when Siobhán appeared in the kitchen. She gently bumped hips with Annie when she passed on her way to the sink. "You look good in my kitchen wearing my shirt," she said with a little wink as she scrubbed her hands to remove the paint.

Annie smiled down at the pan of still-runny eggs and gave them a gentle stir. "Glad you don't mind me taking over."

Siobhán dried her hands and sauntered over. "I'd be a fool to turn down a beautiful woman making me breakfast. You can take over any time you'd like, álainn." She slid her palms along Annie's sides and up under the cotton T-shirt. Her hands were warm and damp as they roamed across Annie's skin. Annie closed her eyes and let the spatula clatter into the skillet as Siobhán toyed with her nipples.

When Siobhán slid a hand into her panties, Annie reached out with shaking fingers to turn off the gas.

"Wet already," Siobhán said as she delved between Annie's lips. It sounded like she was smiling. "I like that."

All Annie could do was moan. Her hips rocked in time with Siobhán's gentle motions and when Siobhán pressed deeper into her, she had to grab for the edge of the counter to anchor herself.

"Oh … oh, God, Siobhán … I'm close," Annie said with a gasp. The incredible number of orgasms from the night before had left her ultra-sensitive and right at the edge.

She could feel the hard pebbles of Siobhán's aroused nipples against her back and the warmth of her breath against Annie's neck. It made her shiver and clench around Siobhán's fingers.

Annie let out a small cry as Siobhán fingered her to a shuddering climax, and after the release ebbed from her, she sagged against Siobhán's body.

She turned her head to kiss Siobhán, feeling weightless from joy.

After they disentangled their bodies. Annie finished cooking, with weak knees and a full heart.

They enjoyed their breakfast at the small table near the window and sat around talking for a long while after. When they finished the coffee, Siobhán made a pot of tea, and Annie accepted a mug with a thank you. She didn't drink it often—mostly because she didn't know what kinds were good—but she'd enjoyed drinking it when she was in Dublin. Annie felt a sense of contentment steal over her as she sat across the little cream-colored wooden table and listened to Siobhán talk about her art. She glowed—from more than just the sun streaming in the windows—and she gestured with her arms, her smile so bright it made Annie feel warm all over.

Siobhán stopped suddenly, and Annie blinked in surprise. "Ugh, listen to me go on," Siobhán said. "Me ma always said I had the gift of the gab, and I'm probably boring you to tears."

Annie chuckled. "Not at all." She paused struggling to find the words to explain why just sitting here and listening to Siobhán talk was enough. "I like this," she finally settled on. "I like being here with you."

Siobhán reached out and squeezed Annie's fingers. "I like it too. My home feels right with you in it."

She stood and gathered the plates, but when Annie tried to help, Siobhán waved her off. "You sit and enjoy your tea. I'll do the washing up."

Annie propped her feet on the other chair and watched Siobhán move gracefully around the kitchen as she put away the dishes and they talked. The scene felt comfortably domestic, and Annie was surprised by how quickly she felt at home in Siobhán's apartment. If Siobhán felt right with Annie in it, Annie could say the same. She felt right being there.

Siobhán gave Annie an apologetic kiss after the kitchen was tidy. "Do you mind if I paint for a bit longer? I'm feeling inspired this morning, and I'd love to keep going for a while." She kissed Annie again, then murmured against her lips, "I think you could be my muse."

"Well how can I refuse that?" Annie commented with a smile.

"You're welcome to anything on my bookshelf or you can borrow my laptop."

"I might do both, thanks." Annie frowned. "Oh, and do you mind if I plug my phone in? I'm sure it's nearly dead."

Siobhán captured her around the waist and pulled her closer. They were both still dressed in just shirts and panties and their bare legs slid together enticingly. "Please, make yourself at home." Unlike when most people said it, Annie had a feeling Siobhán meant that wholeheartedly. It was more than lip service to her.

Siobhán kissed Annie a final time, deeply, then let go with a little sigh. Annie retrieved her phone—completely dead as it turned out—along with the phone charger she always kept stashed in her purse. After plugging it in, she perused Siobhán's bookshelf before settling on a novel by an Irish mystery writer she wasn't familiar with.

She curled up on the couch and drew a soft, cream-colored knit wool throw over her bare legs. Annie had seen similar ones in Ireland, handmade on the Aran Islands, and had been tempted to bring one home with her. She liked the little touches of her birthplace that Siobhán had scattered through her apartment. It was such a beautiful, homey little place.

Annie cracked open the book, but before she began reading, she stole another glance at her new lover. Siobhán gracefully perched on the stool in front of the canvas, staring at it with a look of serious contemplation. She was in profile to Annie, and the sun streaming in the windows lit her from behind and gave her dark hair and pale skin a warm glow. Annie felt like she could stare at Siobhán forever, gorging on her beauty and delicate strength without ever getting sick of it.

Afraid she'd be caught staring or that she'd disturb Siobhán's work, Annie dropped her gaze to the book on her lap. Thankfully, the story was engrossing, and she quickly got lost in it. It wasn't until Siobhán stirred that she looked up again.

"How's the painting going?" she asked quietly.

25

"Quite well," Siobhán answered, rolling her shoulders as if she'd been sitting hunched over for too long. "I'm pleased with it."

"May I see?" Annie was eager for a glimpse of what she'd been working on, but Siobhán shook her head.

"Not quite yet. I'll show you when it's ready." Siobhán turned to look at her. "How's the book?"

"Not bad. Not nearly as nice as watching you though."

Siobhán gave her a half smile. "You flatter me, *álainn*," she murmured.

Annie smiled. "Sorry, I'm probably distracting you."

"I don't mind." Siobhán stretched her arms overhead and leaned forward a little, which made the tank top gap at the neckline, offering Annie a glimpse of the top curve of her breasts. "It's good for me to take a break occasionally."

"I know what you mean. Sometimes, I get so focused on my writing that I lose all track of time, and when I finish, I have knots in my shoulders and a crick in my neck."

Siobhán gave her a smoldering look. "If you're angling for me to give you a massage sometime, it's working."

Annie chuckled. "I wasn't, but I'll keep that in mind. And that goes both ways."

"Mmm." Siobhán's low sound of contentment made Annie's skin tingle, but to her disappointment, Siobhán turned back to the canvas. "I'll paint for a bit longer, then I promise I'll spend the rest of the afternoon with you."

"Take your time," Annie said quietly. "I'm going to get some work done too." Siobhán didn't respond, already immersed in her painting again. Annie stood and stretched, then retrieved the laptop from where it sat on the TV stand. She figured she might as well finish the piece she had due before Siobhán distracted her again.

She took a seat on the couch once more and booted up the laptop. *Crap, I forgot to talk to Siobhán about the password,* she thought. She was about to ask for one, when she realized it had loaded without one.

Siobhán seems to be a very trusting person, Annie thought. She'd opened her home to Annie and offered her the use of her electronics with no thought of Annie snooping through her personal things. Not that she was likely to, even though she'd been given the opportunity, but she appreciated Siobhán's trust.

And, Annie had to admit, it made it easier for her to trust Siobhán. Clearly, Siobhán had nothing to hide.

Annie logged into her email, refreshed her memory about the blog post topic she was supposed to cover, and then quickly brought up a word document and began typing. Unlike many days, the words seemed to flow effortlessly, and in no time at all, Annie had a solid post. She skimmed through the words several more times, tweaking a line here and there, and polishing it until she was sure there were no errors. She saved it and submitted it via email, feeling proud of herself for having gotten her work done with some time to spare. She was forever scrambling to meet deadlines.

When she closed the laptop and set it on the ottoman, she caught sight of Siobhán staring at her with a small smile.

"How'd it go?" she asked.

"Quite well," Annie said, returning the smile. "My work is done."

"As is mine." Siobhán stood gracefully.

"Perfect timing then."

"Want to take a shower?" Siobhán asked, holding out a hand streaked with cobalt and crimson.

"With you?"

Siobhán closed the distance between them and dropped a kiss to Annie's lips before she took her hand. "I wouldn't have it any other way."

Annie closed her eyes as Siobhán slid soapy hands across her skin, massaging her muscles with strong, deft fingers. "God, that feels amazing."

Siobhán nibbled at her ear as their wet skin, slicked with bubbles, rubbed together enticingly. "*You* are amazing."

Annie shook her head, but she was too relaxed to argue.

Siobhán dropped to her knees and ran her hands up Annie's thighs, coaxing Annie to lift one foot onto the edge of the tub. She shifted so her back rested against the corner of the tiled shower, propping herself up.

"Are you good like that?" Siobhán asked, pressing a kiss to Annie's thigh.

Annie reached for the shower curtain rod to anchor herself, grateful it was one of the heavy-duty ones that screwed into the wall. She swallowed hard and nodded. "I'm good."

Siobhán squeezed her ankle, then let go. "Just stay right there, so."

So. Annie smiled. *I haven't heard that since I lived in Dublin. The Irish have a funny habit of ending sentences with 'so' instead of 'then' but it's rather charming ...*

The feel of Siobhán's lips on her pubic mound made Annie's thoughts flee. She gently parted Annie's lips with her fingers and looked up at her. Annie shuddered at the first swipe of her tongue and let her head fall back. She couldn't watch Siobhán go down on her. Not without her legs collapsing out from under her.

Siobhán took her time, exploring Annie's folds with an unhurried thoroughness that made her head spin. Annie felt lightheaded from the heat and steam from the hot water. Along with the feel of Siobhán's tongue, it left her dazed.

Annie cried out when Siobhán eased two fingers into her and began to move them. It took little to tip her over the edge, and after a few short strokes, Annie clenched around Siobhán's fingers, her whole body going tight as she shook from the force of her orgasm.

"Fuck," she cried. "Fuck. I ... *Ohhhhhh.*"

Her legs gave out and the only thing holding her up was her grip on the shower rod. Siobhán stood and pressed her body against Annie's, pinning her to the tile wall. "You okay, love?"

Dazed, Annie lifted her head and opened her eyes. "I'm good." She smiled, feeling drunk and dazed. "So good. I'm not sure my legs will work anymore, but I'm good."

Siobhán chuckled and pressed a kiss against Annie's collarbone. "I promise I won't let you fall."

Annie shakily lowered her foot to the bottom of the tub, then loosened her grip on the curtain rod, flexing her sore fingers, cramped from how hard she'd been clenching it. "That was …" she sighed. "God, Siobhán." "I could do that all day."

"I don't think I could survive you doing that all day," Annie admitted.

Siobhán turned away and reached for a razor, but Annie stilled her. "My turn. Don't move."

Siobhán craned her neck and smiled at her as she let the razor drop into the shower caddy. "Shouldn't I turn around?"

She pressed a kiss to Siobhán's back, right against the little constellation of freckles on her shoulder. "No."

Annie slid her hands around to Siobhán's front, her fingers sliding across her wet skin as she cupped Siobhán's breasts. They felt heavy in her hands, full and soft. Annie brushed her thumbs back and forth across the pebbled tips, feeling the skin crinkle and tighten further. Under the sound of running water, she heard the catch in Siobhán's breathing.

"You like that?" she murmured against Siobhán's ear, and Siobhán nodded. Annie tweaked her rapidly hardening nipples, pinching a little, and Siobhán shuddered, her breath coming hard and fast.

Annie pressed closer to Siobhán, her own breasts rubbing against Siobhán's back. Annie slid one hand lower, over the soft patch of hair, then delved between Siobhán's thighs. She was wet already, her arousal slicker and more silky than the water. Annie cupped her mound in her palm as she slid two fingers into Siobhán's soft heat.

Siobhán's head fell back on Annie's shoulder, and she panted quietly, her hips rising and falling with the rhythm of Annie's touch. Annie gently circled her clit, and Siobhán squirmed against her, increasing the pressure.

"Oh!" Siobhán cried out, sounding surprised. "Oh, Annie," she moaned.

"Like that?" Annie asked, and Siobhán nodded. Annie pressed more tightly to Siobhán, supporting her weight as she fucked Siobhán with her fingers, curling her fingers inward as she pressed hard against her pubic mound and teased Siobhán's nipples.

Siobhán tensed and came apart, shuddering and shaking as she cried out, her hands scrabbling at the slippery tiles. Annie felt a little gush of liquid against her palm, and Siobhán slumped in her arms with a soft cry.

"Easy," Annie murmured, gently withdrawing her fingers.

Siobhán shuddered a final time, and she let her head loll into the curve of Annie's neck.

"*Feck*, Annie," Siobhán murmured dazedly in her ear.

Annie smiled and hugged Siobhán. "Good?"

"Mind-blowing." Siobhán turned in her arms and kissed Annie, a lazy tangle of tongues that conveyed gratitude and happiness.

"You ready to get out?" Annie asked after Siobhán pulled back.

She nodded and turned off the water. Annie pushed back the shower curtain and helped Siobhán out of the tub. She stumbled a little and laughed quietly. "You said I made your legs weak, but mine will hardly hold me."

Thrilled by how thoroughly she'd pleased Siobhán, Annie grabbed a towel from the rack. Siobhán propped herself up against the sink, and Annie dried her, patting her hair dry and gently rubbing at her skin.

Siobhán's head lolled and her eyes went heavy-lidded as she smiled at Annie. "Mmm, this is nice."

Annie smiled back at her. "I'm glad."

"Come back to bed with me?" Siobhán asked as she straightened and took the towel from Annie's hand. "We can nap for a bit, then get up and figure out what we want for dinner."

Annie debated while Siobhán toweled her dry. "I don't know; I really should go home," she finally said.

Siobhán gave her a little pout. "Can't I just have you for a little longer? Spend one more night with me, and I promise I'll let you go home in the morning."

Annie chuckled and kissed her. "And what if you say that again tomorrow?"

"I won't." Siobhán stared at her intently. "I'll be tempted, but I promise I won't pout too much if you want to go home tomorrow."

Annie shook her head, but she let Siobhán drag her back into the bedroom. As Siobhán curled around her and pulled her close, Annie pressed a kiss to her forearm and wondered how she was ever going to convince herself to leave.

Chapter Four

The following day, Annie set her shoes on the mostly empty rack inside the front door of her apartment with a sigh, trying to ignore the tangle of discarded footwear strewn on the wood floor directly next to it. If she let herself get annoyed by every single mess her roommates created, she'd lose her mind.

She'd finally, reluctantly, tore herself from Siobhán's arms to go home. Annie had left her apartment on Friday night and was just now returning on Sunday morning. *Late* morning at that.

She glanced at herself in the mirror, fluffed her hair, and then gave up with a sigh. Almost two days with no grooming products or makeup, besides what she'd had stashed in her purse, and she looked a bit worse for wear. Although, there *was* a well-satisfied glow about her.

Why did she—a fully grown woman—feel like she was doing the walk of shame at the moment. And what did she care what her roommates thought about how she looked *or* acted? That had never mattered to her before. Still, as she maneuvered through the snug living room, filled with Trent's giant TV and oversized couch, she crossed her fingers that everyone would still be in bed or out.

To her chagrin, she ran into Trent and Rebecca as she passed through the large but awkwardly laid out kitchen to get to her bedroom.

"I was starting to wonder if you'd moved out and forgot to tell us," Trent said through a mouthful of food. Annie had been attracted to Trent for about two minutes when they met. He had the kind of square-jawed, tan, preppy handsomeness that a lot of women found attractive, but he'd quickly ruined it for her when he opened his mouth. He wasn't dumb—he had a kinesiology degree and worked as a physical therapist—he was just kind of a jackass.

"Nope," Annie said. "Just went out."

He raised an eyebrow at her. "For two days?" When she didn't reply, he whistled lowly. "Oh, I get it. It was a date."

Rebecca—who had been sitting in a chair with her knees drawn up while she painted her toes—glanced up, nail polish brush frozen in her hand. "You had a date?"

"It wasn't really a date," Annie protested.

"I thought you went to a gallery show on Friday night." Rebecca capped the nail polish bottle and twisted it shut. Her pretty face screwed up in confusion.

"I did. But I didn't go to the gallery show with anyone. I just went by myself."

"So what'd you do, fall asleep in the gallery and not wake up until now?" Trent asked.

Annie cracked a smile. "No. I didn't sleep at the gallery. I ... met someone there. The artist, actually. We really hit it off."

"Oooh," Rebecca's brown eyes sparkled. "Is he cute?"

"He must have been good in bed at least," Trent added. "If you were gone for two days."

She cleared her throat. "*She*, actually."

Rebecca twisted her thick, curly brown hair up into a messy bun using the elastic on her wrist. She glanced at Annie when she was done. "Oh, right. I forget about that."

"That" meaning her bisexuality.

Rebecca looked back down at her toes as if she was bored now that the conversation wasn't about a guy. Rebecca had always been nice, but they didn't have much in common. She was the quintessential Boston white girl, complete with Ugg boots and North Face jackets. She'd dated a string of guys in the time Annie had known her, jumping from relationship to relationship in a never-ending search for the perfect man. Despite living together, their lives were worlds apart, and Annie probably shouldn't have been surprised that Rebecca didn't quite understand her bisexuality.

33

"Her name is Siobhán," Annie said aloud. "She's an amazing painter, and we really clicked."

"What kind of a name is that?" Trent asked. "Is she some weird hippy chick? Or black? Because Sha-vonn kinda sounds like she might be."

"The name *Siobhán* is Irish. And you probably don't want to try to guess how it's spelled. I can pretty much guarantee you'd be wrong." Annie crossed her arms over her chest. "Besides, Dee is black. Why would you of all people *care* if I'm dating a black woman?" Dee was Trent's girlfriend and the fourth roommate in their three-bedroom apartment.

"I don't. I just didn't know you were down with that."

"Right." Annie rolled her eyes and walked toward her bedroom.

"So I have to ask. Is your tongue tired from all the pussy-eating you did?" Trent asked. "I would get so sick of that."

Annie turned back to face him. "You're dating a woman—you should know what it's like."

"Yeah, but I've got a dick." Trent grabbed his crotch through the thin fabric of his athletic shorts. "I don't have to use my tongue much. Just on special occasions, like her birthday."

"Dee is such a lucky woman," Annie replied, rolling her eyes again. Frankly, Dee was way too smart for Trent, but there was no accounting for taste. Dee was also in nursing school and so busy with her clinical rotations that Annie rarely saw them together. Maybe that was how the relationship worked? Either that or Trent was stellar in bed. After all, why else would Dee put up with his obnoxiousness?

Trent smirked. "You know it, baby. What I'm packing is way better than that hunk of plastic you probably strap on."

Annie opened her mouth, but no words came out. Instead, she turned and made a beeline for her bedroom. Probably better not to get into a discussion about what sex between two women was like. At best, Trent would claim that it wasn't real sex without a dick involved. At worst, he'd ask her to demonstrate it for him.

She firmly shut the door behind her with a sense of relief. *Jesus, if I don't strangle that guy one day, it will be a fucking miracle.*

Annie squeezed by her bed, retrieved her phone from her purse, and hung it on a hook next to the minuscule closet. She turned around to look at her bedroom, and the view made her frown.

The room was hardly big enough to turn around in. She'd managed to cram in a comfy, full size bed and shelf and chair combo that functioned as a desk of sorts, but there was little space for anything else. Annie sighed and fell back onto the lavender duvet. Her room was as neat as she could make it with so little space, and she'd painted and hung a couple art prints on the walls to spruce it up, but the more she looked at it, the more it came up lacking. Siobhán's apartment hadn't been large but it had been bright and welcoming. Compared to that, Annie's room felt bland and lifeless.

Especially without a gorgeous Irish woman in my bed, Annie mused.

She'd left Siobhán's place reluctantly, but she was determined not to overstay her welcome. And now that she was home, she felt blah and had begun to regret leaving. It had all just been such a whirlwind—meeting Siobhán, hitting it off so well, climbing into bed, and barely leaving it for two days—and so impulsive. So un-Annie. She'd loved every minute of it, but it really wasn't her style.

What was that old joke about lesbians moving in together after two dates? Well, maybe it was because she was bi or just because she'd had her heart broken a time or six—by women *and* men—but she couldn't quite move that fast. She needed some time to re-group and think.

Annie sighed and stared at the ceiling for a while, watching the sunlight filter through the leaves of the tree outside her window make pretty patterns on the ceiling. It was the best part of living here. The apartment itself was nothing special, and Annie really could have done without the hassle of sharing it with three other people, but she had fallen in love with the way the sun streamed through her bedroom windows. Whenever she felt stressed, she liked to lie on the bed and let her mind drift as she watched the light play through the trees.

If it wouldn't involve Siobhán having to deal with her obnoxious roommates, Annie would bring Siobhán there and show her. She could picture lying naked in bed with Siobhán, watching the sunlight shift and move as they talked.

Annie rolled over onto her stomach with a sigh when she realized she and Siobhán hadn't done a lot of getting to know each other. Well, they had *physically*, but she'd only gotten little snippets about where Siobhán had come from and what her past was like. They'd ignored that part in favor of more physical things.

When she'd left Siobhán's place, Siobhán had kissed her goodbye and promised they'd talk soon. But they hadn't made any official plans to get together again. Or talked about what they wanted. Earlier, as Annie took the subway home to the North End, her fears and insecurities had multiplied until the entire weekend with Siobhán had seemed like a beautiful dream she'd woken up from. Which meant it would gradually fade until it was nothing but a memory.

Now, doubts assailed Annie. Had this just been a fling for Siobhán? Did Siobhán do this often? Maybe she regularly brought home women she met at her shows and went to bed with them for two days.

Annie groaned and rolled onto her back again before she forced herself to get up and take a seat at her so-called desk. Freaking out about Siobhán wasn't going to get her anywhere. She might as well see if she could get any more work done. Aside from the one blog post, her life had been more or less put on hold for two days. Now that she was home, she needed to get back to it.

Annie checked her email and was disappointed to find no new freelance opportunities. She checked her bank balance, which only made her more depressed. She'd just gotten home, intending to be productive, and now all she wanted to do was leave. Or crawl under the covers and pretend like her life wasn't a pathetic mess.

Determined to shake herself out of the funk she was in, Annie forced herself to do some work. She spent a while reading articles on freelancing tips. Then searched for new sites to find jobs on. She cleaned out her email inbox and spent a while wandering social media and liking all of the exciting things her friends and acquaintances were up to. Her own posts were usually quite boring. Mostly funny memes and the occasional news article.

Annie laughed to herself as she thought about posting about meeting Siobhán Murray the artist and going to bed with her. Now *that* would get some reactions. Annie found herself searching for Siobhán and quickly located her artist page and what appeared to be a more personal profile. It was filled with interactions with people, information about her shows and current projects, and—worst of all—Siobhán posing in pictures with several beautiful women. Annie couldn't help the sense of relief when she saw that none of the pictures were terribly recent.

She groaned and closed out of the site before she made herself even crazier than she already was. She closed her laptop lid, got comfy on the bed, and turned on the TV. She flipped through TV channels, briefly pausing on a home décor show, but it didn't hold her interest, and she found herself getting distracted.

Hunger finally drove her out of her room.

Thankfully, her roommates had vacated the kitchen. Unfortunately, they hadn't cleaned up after themselves. Annie doubted any cleaning had been done since she left on Friday. In fact, she was sure there was a pile of dishes on the counter that had been in the exact same position for days.

Rebecca only ate microwaved freezer meals—usually the low fat, low sodium type that tasted like cardboard to Annie—and Dee was never home long enough to eat, so the kitchen should have stayed neat enough. Annie always cleaned up after herself. But Rebecca left dirty forks everywhere, along with a trashcan constantly overflowing with the boxes and trays from her meals.

Trent was the biggest culprit though. He was always blending protein shakes and prepping healthy food for the week, which would have been fine if he didn't put off washing his dishes as long as possible. It was why there was a sink and countertop full of them. And a weird smell in the air.

Annie grimaced and pulled heavy rubber gloves on. She gingerly piled Trent's dishes in one basin of the sink before she pulled out the bleach spray. She nearly choked on the fumes, and her eyes watered as she scrubbed the remnants clinging to the sides and bottom. But it was better than gagging at the smell of spoiled food.

She rinsed the sink and her gloves thoroughly before washing the pan she needed. It took a while to scrape the bits of baked on food from the bottom, and by the time she finally did, she was grumpy and no longer motivated to cook dinner.

She rinsed out the pan, set it in the drainer to dry, and stripped off the gloves, glad to have the disgusting job done.

In deference to her rumbling stomach, she heated a can of soup and grabbed an apple from the fruit bowl and called it good.

When she returned to her bedroom, she noticed a light on her phone flashing with a notification.

She put her food on the nightstand and picked up her phone, torn between hope it was from Siobhán and anxiety that it would just be a text reminder to pick up her birth control prescription. She smiled when she saw it *was* a message from Siobhán.

Hey, beautiful the text read.

Annie smiled. *Hey, yourself. Sorry, I was making dinner and cleaning up.*

How was your day? came the prompt reply.

I probably should have just stayed at your place, Annie admitted, her fingers flying over the screen of her phone. *My roommates are jackasses, my bedroom is tiny, and you weren't in it.*

That's your first lesson in dating Siobhán Murray. I am always right about such things.

Should I keep that in mind for the future? Annie replied.

Absolutely, was the swift response.

Annie's heart soared when she realized this was definitely not the end of things with Siobhán.

It seemed her fears had been totally unfounded.

Siobhán sent her another message, and they texted back and forth for a while as Annie ate her dinner.

In fact, they texted all evening until Annie could hardly keep her eyes open. Eventually, she sleepily typed goodnight to Siobhán and muted her phone.

She flipped on her side and hugged a pillow close as she thought about the date she had with Siobhán the following Tuesday night.

She fell asleep thinking about Siobhán's long dark hair, soft lips, and the murmur of an Irish accent in her ear.

Chapter Five
July

Annie fussed with her hair in the mirror by the door before straightening with a sigh. It would have to do.

"I told you, you look fine." Rebecca rolled her eyes, but her tone was surprisingly kind. Annie had come to her in desperation a little earlier, asking for help with her outfit. Annie had expected Rebecca to blow her off, but she'd been rather sweet and helpful. She'd even loaned Annie a necklace.

"Says the woman who owns more styling products than the salon she works at and spends more time getting ready to go to the gym than I spend getting ready for my date?" Annie teased.

"That means you should listen to me. I obviously know what I'm talking about. Which is obviously why you came to me in the first place." Rebecca's tone was lofty, but she offered Annie a smile. "Come here."

She fluffed the hair at Annie's scalp, then tweaked the curls a little. "There."

Annie glanced in the mirror again. "Thanks. That is better."

"Told you." Rebecca's tone was smug. "Have fun tonight."

"Thanks."

"Is it a date with Shi—ugh, whatever your girlfriend's name is?"

"Siobhán. Yes." Girlfriend was debatable since they hadn't actually officially discussed the exclusivity or labels things yet, but there was no point in correcting Rebecca's assumption.

"Things are going well, huh?"

"Yeah, they are." Annie smiled. "I've been really happy."

"I can tell." Rebecca smiled back at her. "I still don't get the whole occasional lesbian thing, but whatever."

Annie took a deep breath and bit back an instinctive retort, wanting to keep things civil. "Thanks for the help with my hair, Rebecca. Have a good night."

"You too. Or, however long you're there!"

"Thanks."

It's true, Annie thought as she closed the door behind her. *And I really can't get too mad at Rebecca for teasing me about it. I have been spending a lot of time at Siobhán's in the past couple weeks, and I only come home every few days.*

She hadn't bothered to invite Siobhán to her place. Siobhán's apartment was cleaner, quieter, and—most importantly—*private.*

Things with Siobhán had been going incredibly well. Over the past two weeks, she and Siobhán had spent a good chunk of time discovering the city. Annie was a bit of a history buff, and Siobhán hadn't spent much time exploring early American history, so they'd been doing it together. They'd spent an afternoon walking the Freedom Trail that ran from Boston Common to the bridge in Charleston, with the USS Constitution and the Bunker Hill Monument, and passed sixteen of the city's historic monuments and sights.

They'd also spent an evening at Faneuil Hall—a city market hall from the 1700s—wandering the shops, restaurants, and exhibitions there.

After that, they'd gone to a restaurant that Siobhán claimed served the best fish and chips on this side of the Atlantic. Annie was inclined to agree.

They'd talked about going to Boston Common to see the swan boats and walk through the park. And planned a day at the Harvard Art Museum, along with the other museums scattered throughout Boston.

They'd spent most of those nights together as well, and they certainly hadn't grown bored with their time in bed together. Siobhán was a creative and enthusiastic lover, and Annie had never felt so satisfied.

She was falling hard and fast for Siobhán, but she hadn't quite worked up the courage to ask Siobhán if she was feeling the same way.

Annie glanced at her phone when she reached the street, relieved to see that the Lyft car she'd splurged on to save her a mile walk in heels would be there any moment. She arrived at a bistro near the Navy Yard just as Siobhán strolled up.

"Hello, beautiful." Siobhán greeted her with a kiss, either completely unaware or unconcerned about the people around them who might be watching.

"Hey," Annie smiled at her. Siobhán looked stylish and comfortable in a sleek navy sheath dress, nude heels, an emerald green belt, and a colorful scarf. Annie had cobbled together an appropriate outfit from a black skirt she'd worn to a wedding a few years back, the white button-down shirt she'd worn to several interviews, and the statement necklace Rebecca had loaned her. But Annie was envious of Siobhán's effortlessly chic look.

"Are you ready to go in?" Siobhán asked. "I made a reservation."

"Absolutely. I'm starved."

Siobhán led the way inside and checked in with the hostess. "Two. Under the name of Siobhán Murray."

"I have a 'See-o-ban Murray' listed," the woman said brightly. "Is that it?"

Siobhán sigh heavily. "That's me. It's an unusual spelling."

A waitress led them out to a shaded table on the patio, introduced herself, and took their orders for wine and water.

"This is what I get for making reservations online," Siobhán said drily when she was gone. "You'd think I'd learn."

"Has it been a huge hassle since you moved here?" Annie asked. "To the US, I mean."

Siobhán shrugged. "It's occasionally tiring, but there are a lot of Irish ex-pats and Irish-Americans here in Boston. It's better than it would be in Kansas." She exchanged a smile with Annie. "Besides, I keep at it with the ones who aren't familiar with it. I taught my name to a whole class once. I took a few courses shortly after I got here, and we had guest artists come in and teach occasionally. One of them butchered my name, and in unison the whole class spoke up and said, 'It's *Shi-vonn*'."

41

Annie's laugh was loud and genuine, and for the first time all day, she found herself relaxing. She'd spent the day stressing about money and her future, and it was a relief to let it all go and just enjoy being with Siobhán.

The waitress returned with their drinks, and Siobhán leaned in when she left. "Anyway, that's enough of my prattling on about my name. How are you?"

"Better now that I'm here," Annie admitted. Siobhán reached out to touch her hand. "How's your week going?"

Siobhán shrugged. "Pretty well. I'm making great progress on the piece I was working on. Gabriel's ecstatic about the way the collection seems to be coming together, and, frankly, so am I." She took a sip of her wine. "How about you? How's your work going?"

"I'm trying to drum up some more freelance jobs but not having a lot of luck. Things seem to be drying up."

Siobhán frowned. "We could have rescheduled if you needed to spend some more time on that."

"Thanks. Honestly, though, I was glad to get out," Annie admitted. "I was feeling stir-crazy, which leaves me with no patience for dealing with my roommates."

"How'd you end up living with them anyway?"

Annie shrugged. "The usual, I guess. No money, high rent prices."

"Boston, Dublin, they're all the same when it comes to finding a place to live," Siobhán said with a rueful sigh. "Still, it beats living in a place in the middle of nowhere. Cheap, but nothing to do and no one to do it with."

"Right? I grew up in Concord, and I've thought about moving back out into the suburbs but the thought depresses me." She shrugged. "Anyway, in this case, I was in a relationship with this guy Mark. He made good money working for some tech company, so we lived here in the North End. I liked the area, but after we broke up, the only way I could afford it was to sublet a room in an apartment with a few other people. There was an ad on Craigslist, and the place was decent enough for the price."

"Should I be worried about you when you're there?" Siobhán said with a frown.

"No. They're not *terrible*," Annie admitted. "I mean, I feel safe there, and they don't break my things, unlike one of my roommates from college. Trent 'borrows'"—Annie made finger quotes—"my butter all the time, and I'm always turning up short when I go to make toast, but it's not that serious. They get on my nerves, but I can live with it. Pun not intended."

Siobhán grimaced. "Still. It's kind of miserable."

"It really is," Annie agreed. She took a sip of her water and glanced down at her menu. "I suppose we should figure out our order."

"Yes," Siobhán said with a soft laugh. "It seems I get so wrapped up in you that I lose track of everything else."

Annie smiled. Siobhán certainly wasn't the only one.

A short while later, the waitress returned and took their orders. Over an appetizer of steamed clams, Annie brought up the picture on Siobhán's fridge.

"That reminds me, I keep meaning to ask where you went clam digging." Siobhán gave her a quizzical glance. "I assumed that's what you were doing in the photo in your kitchen anyway."

"*Oh.*" Siobhán sighed. "I went with my ex-girlfriend Laura. Her family had a place on the Outer Banks. They were very old money, and the family dug clams when they felt like playing the peasant." Her tone was scornful.

Annie shrugged. "They couldn't have been all bad if they invited their daughter's partner to go with them."

Siobhán took a swig of her wine and frowned. "That's what I thought. Until I got there and realized they thought Laura and I were roommates. *Platonic* roommates. They had no idea we'd been living together—in sin—for the better part of two years. And she certainly did nothing to inform them otherwise."

Annie winced. "If it was so terrible, why do you keep the photo on your refrigerator?"

She smiled grimly and dug the clam meat out of the shell with a vicious stab of her seafood fork. "I enjoyed the clam digging. And it's a reminder to myself about what I want to stay away from."

43

"Women with conservative families?" Annie asked. She dipped a piece of sourdough bread into the garlicky wine broth the clams had been steamed in.

"Self-loathing lesbians who pretend they're bisexual to appease their own guilt about letting down the family."

Annie winced. Siobhán reached out and touched her hand. "I'm sorry, Annie. I know you're not that type of person, but you must admit, there are plenty of women out there like that."

"Some, yes," Annie agreed. "But I think painting us all with the same broad brush does more damage than good."

Siobhán sighed. "You're probably right. But there's only so many times I can get my heart broken before I flinch when a woman says she's bi."

"Not all bi women are like Laura," Annie argued.

"I know that, Annie. But she's hardly the only one. And she took a very long time to get over. We fought on that vacation with her family. I came home, someone came to collect Laura's things, and I never saw her again. Except in the newspaper when they announced her engagement to the man of her dreams." Siobhán expression turned sour. "The last I heard, they were living in a huge place in Back Bay with a couple of children, and her husband was well on his way toward a political career."

Annie winced. "I'm sorry, Siobhán. I can't imagine how painful that must have been."

She offered Annie a wan smile. "You don't want to know how many times I've thought about doing a tell-all book and selling the paintings I did of Laura and I together to the highest bidder. It would be such perfect revenge, and do you know what it would do for my sales?" Siobhán sighed. "But I could never live with myself."

Annie took Siobhán's hand. "I understand the urge though."

"Anyway." Siobhán picked up her fork to attack the clams again. "That's ancient history."

Is it though? Annie wondered. Somehow, she wasn't so sure.

They finished their appetizer in silence. It grew oppressive after the waitress cleared away their dishes. Uncomfortable and unsure what to say, Annie looked out over the patio. It was shady, and the wind coming off the water was a fresh, salty breeze that stirred the humid summer air. If only the tension would dissipate so easily. She glanced back at Siobhán, who sat across the table from her, frowning.

"Annie, I—"

"Don't worry about it," Annie said gently. "We can talk more later. This isn't really the time or place."

Siobhán nodded.

A few moments later, the waitress returned with the entrees, and Annie felt a sense of relief. Food occupied them for a few minutes as they tucked into their meals.

"How's your roasted mushroom risotto?" Siobhán asked after she'd taken a few bites.

"Delicious," Annie said. "Your miso cod?"

"Amazing. Thanks."

They managed to find less contentious topics as they finished their lunch, but after, they hit another small bump.

The waitress left the bill on the table after they'd declined dessert, and Annie opened her purse to get her wallet.

"Oh, I've got it," Siobhán said as she reached for it.

"Are you sure?" Annie asked.

"Of course." Siobhán smiled at her. "The gallery show went well, and things are moving forward with the commissioned work. Let me treat you."

"You've been paying for almost everything in the past few weeks," Annie argued.

Siobhán leaned forward and touched her hand. "I appreciate the gesture, Annie, but I know you're not in the best place with your career now and I am. What harm does it cause for me to treat you?"

"None, I suppose." Annie smiled at Siobhán and squeezed her hand. "Thank you."

Siobhán's smile was bright. "Now, how about we go out for a drink? My treat as well."

"That sounds nice," Annie said.

"Good. I know just the place, so."

Chapter Six

Annie had never been to the bar Siobhán took her to. But it appeared Siobhán was a regular. The hostess greeted Siobhán with a smile and a kiss on the cheek, and one of the waitresses waved as they crossed to sit by the sleek marble bar. The interior was cozy and elegant, with dim lighting and mellow music.

"Come here often?" Annie asked, amused. She took a seat on the leather bar stool and hung her purse on the hook near her knee.

Siobhán shrugged as she settled onto the stool beside Annie. "It's been a while, actually. I dated a woman who tended bar here." Annie raised an eyebrow, and Siobhán laughed. "She's moved out of state. I wouldn't bring you to a place where an ex currently worked. I think I've had my fill of making things awkward when it comes to my exes this evening, thank you."

Annie chuckled softly and reassured her. "It's not a big deal. I run into my exes occasionally. Boston is a big city, but it's not *that* big."

"I suppose that's true."

"What can I get you, ladies?"

Annie looked up and met the eye of the bartender. He was young and good looking, with hair almost as dark as Siobhán's. "Oh, I haven't even had a chance to look at what you have," Annie admitted.

He slid a cocktail menu toward her, smiled, and gave her a little wink. "Whatever the lady wants."

Annie refrained from rolling her eyes as she looked down at the menu.

"Tullamore Dew. Twelve year. Neat," Siobhán said crisply.

"A lady who knows her whiskeys." The bartender sounded impressed.

47

"In my family, I woulda been disowned if I didn't." Siobhán laid on the accent thickly, and Annie smiled down at her menu. "Do you need another minute, Annie?"

She looked up. "No. I'll take a grapefruit basil martini, please."

"Coming right up." The bartender turned away to fix their drinks, and Annie glanced at Siobhán. "That sounds like quite a story there. Would your family really disown you if you didn't know your whiskeys?"

"Nah. My uncle owns a pub. He *is* terribly fond of his whiskeys, but I may have exaggerated a bit." Siobhán's nonchalant shrug made Annie laugh. "Anyway, before the bartender came up, we were talking about how small the community is. I was going to ask if you stayed friends with any of your exes."

Annie nodded. "With a few. Usually the ones who I was somewhat friends with before we started sleeping together. And never the ones who broke my heart." She tried to remember the last time she'd seen any of them in person and failed. Well, maybe they were more acquaintances than friends these days.

Siobhán smiled ruefully. "I changed universities to avoid one of mine. And I had to retake a term's worth of classes to do it."

"Really?"

"I needed a fresh start," Siobhán said. When she didn't elaborate, Annie bit her tongue to keep from asking why. If she wanted to, Siobhán would share it. Annie couldn't imagine any breakup that ended with uprooting her life at a university was a good one. Besides, they'd clearly stumbled onto a minefield during dinner when the subject of Laura had come up. Annie wasn't about to risk it again. How many exes did Siobhán have? And how deep were the scars they'd left?

"Here you go, ladies." The bartender placed their drinks in front of them. "My name's Chad if you need anything. And I do mean *anything*."

Siobhán rolled her eyes at Annie, but thankfully, someone called for him at the other end of the bar and he left with a wink.

She took a sip of her drink and instantly forgave Chad the bartender. A little obnoxious? Yes. But he mixed a mean drink. And Annie could definitely forgive Siobhán for taking her to a place where her ex-girlfriend had worked. Clearly, the drinks were worth it.

48

"This cocktail is amazing. I can see why you keep coming here," Annie admitted.

"That's why I brought you here," Siobhán said. "I rarely order cocktails, but I knew they had a good selection all around."

"Do you go out a lot?" Annie asked.

Siobhán raised an eyebrow at her, and she hastily explained, "Not on dates. I mean, do you check out the nightlife in Boston a lot?" Annie waved her arm to indicate the kind of place they were in. "Bars, restaurants, that sort of thing."

"Fairly often. Although, I go to gallery openings and art benefits more. Places where I can network and meet the right people. It's all part of the job." She gave Annie a puzzled look. "Why do you ask?"

"Oh, you just seem to know all the great places in the area, and, uh, your social media made it seem as though you were out a lot," Annie said with a sheepish look, slightly embarrassed to admit it. "I was, um, stalking you online a little."

Siobhán laughed loud enough to draw the attention of people near them at the bar, then leaned in and lowered her voice. "Well, you are very difficult to stalk. You have everything set to private."

Annie grinned, relieved.

"Oh, that reminds me. Shall we take a selfie and plaster it all over social media? It seems to be the thing to do when one is dating someone new." She retrieved her phone and played with it for a moment.

Chuckling, Annie agreed. "Sure, why not?"

Siobhán shifted in her seat and wrapped an arm around Annie's shoulders, holding the camera up and out so they were both visible on the screen. "Say cheese," she joked.

Siobhán took several shots, and when she showed them to Annie, she picked the second one. "That one, definitely." Her smile looked more natural, and she liked the way Siobhán held her close.

"That's my favorite as well." Siobhán shot her a small smile. "Now, I'll have to add you on all the social media platforms so I can tag you."

"Dating in the twenty-first century is such fun," Annie joked.

"Well, it beats being a lesbian in the nineteenth century, I suppose," Siobhán said with a wry smile as her fingers flew over her screen. Annie's phone buzzed with notifications, and she quickly accepted Siobhán's requests.

"There was always the Boston marriage," she countered.

Siobhán frowned. "I'm not familiar with the term."

Annie brightened. "Oh, in the nineteenth and early twentieth century, there were some women—usually the suffragette types—who lived together. They had independent income and no children. I don't know how many of them there actually were, and historians are kind of mixed on how many of them were lesbians, but it sounds like a few were fairly forthright about sharing a bed."

"Fascinating." Siobhán looked up from her phone. "I'd like to learn more about that."

"I know Henry James wrote a novel about it because his sister was living with a woman. I read the book in college, but I can't remember the name off the top of my head. It had something to do with Boston because his sister and her partner lived here. That's where the term came from. You should read it."

"I'd love to! That sounds so interesting!" Siobhán set her phone down on the bar.

"Really? I'm not boring you to tears with my history and literature talk?" Annie said drily.

"No, not at all." Siobhán took a sip of her drink.

Annie's phone buzzed in her hand, and she took a peek at the posts Siobhán had tagged her in. The sight made Annie smile. She'd expected Siobhán would seem completely out of her league, but they looked good together. Light and dark. Balanced.

"Have you ever thought about doing something related to history for a career?"

Annie shrugged and stashed her phone in her purse again. "The thought has crossed my mind, but it's really more of a hobby than a career. I don't want to teach."

"Hmm, well, strike that off the list then." Siobhán hummed thoughtfully. "You mentioned that you were disillusioned with journalism by the time you got in the field. Why is that? I've been meaning to ask you about it."

She sighed. "Well, I grew up here in the Boston area and went to Northeastern. They have a great journalism program where you work for a newspaper while you go to school. I worked for a smaller daily newspaper—The Boston Chronicle—and I was so sure I was going to love hunting down the next big story and getting the big scoop, but it turns out, I hated it. I had real life experience by the time I graduated, but I was already disillusioned with the field by the time I had my degree."

"How so?"

"I loved the writing itself, the field just ... wasn't what I had imagined. For one, journalism isn't like it used to be. Reporters are being asked to do more work with fewer resources and staff. You're not just a reporter; you're a digital storyteller. You have to be able to shoot photos and videos yourself and package them all into a finished project. And there's this constant pressure to make the news more sensational, more attention-grabbing." Annie looked down. "I had this idealistic idea of what journalism would be. I think I was naïve."

Siobhán made a face. "I would hate that."

"I kept hearing horror stories from friends too. One friend worked for a small town newspaper after graduation. He was trying to do good work, but people were hostile toward the paper for shining too much light on the 'good ole boy' networks. He was sued by a corrupt building official who was trying to cover his tracks. They settled after six years because the paper didn't want to pay to go to trial, but it really turned him off on the field, and he quit shortly after."

"How horrible."

Annie nodded. "Stories like that didn't exactly fuel my passion for journalism. Plus, I hated the lifestyle. You have to drop everything if there's a big fire or a crime bust, no matter what time of day. After a few years of working for the Chronicle, I was exhausted, and I dreaded going into work every day."

Siobhán smiled sympathetically. "I can see how that would be draining."

"It was." Annie took another sip of her cocktail. "If it's something I love, I'll work myself to the bone and make all the necessary sacrifices, but it was very difficult to do that for a career I didn't even enjoy. If that had been the only thing, I probably would have learned to deal with it, but I'd lost my passion. I didn't feel like I was contributing anything good to the world. But, it was hard to quit and admit I'd failed."

"There's no shame in admitting when something doesn't work for you."

"Oh, I suppose. But it was humiliating to admit that I didn't want anything to do with the degree I'd invested so much time and effort into."

"How was your family about it?"

Annie shrugged. "My mother was annoyed and said 'you'd better not come to us begging for more money.' My dad just frowned a lot and looked disappointed in me. That was the worst."

Siobhán's frown was sympathetic. "Not very supportive."

"No, but they'd paid a good amount of money on tuition and room and board—not to mention a semester abroad in Ireland—so I can't blame them too much."

"Mmm, yes, the American education system is appalling. I don't know how you stand it."

"I think most of us feel like we have no choice," Annie said drily. She leaned forward. "If you've stayed in Boston for this long, you must like it here though. The U.S., I mean."

"Oh, I do. I've thought about moving back to Ireland, but it's definitely easier to be a lesbian here in the States. At least in Boston. You have some strange religious groups in various parts of the country, but there's still less of a stranglehold on the general population than the Catholic Church has in Ireland."

"Even now?"

Siobhán's smile was bitter. "Abortion is still illegal in The Republic of Ireland and Northern Ireland, Annie. Women have to travel to England or Wales to have it done. And if they can't afford that, they have to find a way to self-induce. Or carry it to term and put it up for adoption. I've never had to worry about it myself but friends …" Siobhán shook her head. "It's barbaric."

Annie winced. "That's wretched."

"It is. The history of the way the church treated women in Ireland would make your hair curl," Siobhán said. She stared thoughtfully down into her glass as she swirled the remaining amber-colored liquor in it before she took another sip.

"I can imagine."

"Ireland's a beautiful country, but it has an ugly side too. Most places do, I suppose, but it doesn't make it better."

"The U.S. has quite an ugly side too," Annie agreed. "I wish I'd learned more about that sort of thing in Ireland when I went for the study abroad though," she admitted. "Unfortunately, I was young and way more interested in having fun."

"I wasn't terribly socially aware when I was at university either," Siobhán said drily. "I think you can be forgiven."

"Can I get you ladies anything else?" Annie glanced away from Siobhán to see Chad staring at them expectantly.

Annie glanced down at her martini glass. There was only a sip or two left. "Sure, I'll take another one of these."

"Me as well," Siobhán said, holding up her nearly empty glass.

"Tullamore Dew again?"

"Please."

"Sure thing."

"Sorry to bring the mood down tonight," Siobhán said when he disappeared to get their drinks.

"I don't mind," Annie said, surprised by Siobhán's apology. "I'm enjoying myself."

"If you're sure." Siobhán sounded a little doubtful.

Annie reached out and touched Siobhán's forearm. "I want to get to know you. That's not always going to be the light, easy conversations."

"True enough."

"Besides, I like how passionate you are," Annie said. "About everything. It's refreshing."

She'd dated too many bland, boring people in her life. People who were more concerned about getting along than having an opinion. Siobhán was a breath of fresh air.

An hour and another drink later, Siobhán laid a hand on Annie's arm. "I don't know about you, but I'm about ready to head out. I don't think I can wait any longer to get my hands on you."

Annie flushed, the alcohol and Siobhán's proximity and raw sexuality making her head swim. Siobhán had been relentlessly—if subtly—flirting with her since they got their second drinks. "Me either."

Siobhán leaned in and spoke directly in her ear. "I may not even make it to the bedroom. I may spread you out on my couch and feast on your cunt right there."

Annie bit back a moan. Apparently, subtlety had gone out the window with Siobhán's second drink. "Yeah. We *definitely* need to go now then."

Siobhán gave her a knowing little smile. "I'll get the bill."

"I'm going to run to the restroom while you do."

"Better not come yet, love."

Annie laughed softly, but she felt a thrill run through her anyway. "I wasn't planning to get myself off *here*, Siobhán."

"Good. That's my job."

Annie stood, her knees a little wobbly, but she wasn't sure if that was from the drinks or Siobhán's potent words.

She made her way unsteadily across the bar to the restroom and made quick work of her business there. Her hands were still slightly damp from the hasty towel drying she'd done when she emerged.

54

She was so lost in thought about what would happen with Siobhán as soon as they got back to her place that she almost ran into someone in the hallway.

"Sorry," she said with a gasp, looking up to realize it was Chad.

"No worries. You can mow me down anytime," he joked.

Flustered and unsure how to respond, Annie moved to skirt around him, but he blocked her path with his arm. "Hey, hold up for a second. I couldn't help checking you out earlier." He smiled, showing his dimples. "You said you didn't have any plans tonight, so I was wondering if you'd like to go do something. I just got off shift."

Annie cleared her throat, annoyed by the interruption. She just wanted to get to Siobhán and go home. "Uhh, well, I'm here on a date already with that gorgeous woman I was sitting next to at the bar," she pointed out.

He frowned. "Sorry. You just didn't seem like—" Annie braced herself for the inevitable "dyke" or "butch" comment. "—you were on a date," he finished. "I thought maybe you were just good friends. I mean, it's so hard to tell with women, you know?"

"I could have stuck my tongue down her throat while we were sitting at the bar," Annie said, the snarky response slipping out before she could stop herself. "Would that have helped?"

He smirked at her. "Well, I mean, I wouldn't mind watching—or more—if you two were into that. She's pretty hot too."

Annie stifled a sigh. And there it was. The inevitable comment about a threesome. She'd had a few in her life and enjoyed them at the time, but she was tired that men always assumed she'd be up for one. And even if Siobhán were attracted to men, Annie couldn't fathom sharing Siobhán with anyone. "We're not into that," she said shortly. "And I'm not into you."

He stepped back and ran a hand through his hair. "Look, I'm sorry. I didn't mean to offend you."

Annie did sigh aloud now. "Can I go now, please?" She brushed past him and saw Siobhán standing nearby. Her expression darkened as Annie approached.

"What was that about?" Siobhán slid a hand around her waist.

"Let's just get out of here. I'll explain it when we get back to your place."

Siobhán frowned but nodded in agreement. She guided Annie out the door, and they walked in silence the few short blocks to Siobhán's apartment.

Annie had barely closed the door behind her when Siobhán rounded on her. "What happened at the bar?"

"Nothing serious," Annie tried to brush it off. "Chad hit on me, is all. I was more annoyed by his assumption that we weren't on a date than anything else." She dropped her purse onto the floor near the door and took off her shoes. "And him angling for a threesome."

"Ugh. That's the problem with dating bi women," Siobhán muttered.

"Well, you're hardly the stereotypical lesbian either," Annie snapped as she straightened. She crossed her arms over her chest. "You must get hit on by men all the time."

Siobhán grimaced. "More of them than I'd like, that's for sure. But that's not the point. You confuse them."

"*I* confuse them? How?"

"You give off vibes."

"Oh, I'm sorry. Do I give off some kind of waves that confuse people's gaydar?"

"That's not what I meant, Annie."

"No, this is bullshit. I don't know why you're sulking about this. I had no control over him hitting on me. Nor do I have control over whom I'm attracted to!" Annie snapped.

"I can't stand the thought of anyone else touching you."

"Have I ever said I *want* anyone else to touch me?" Annie argued. "I can't think about anyone but you, Siobhán!"

"Good." Siobhán yanked Annie to her and kissed her deeply, her mouth hot and damp. The kiss was forceful, claiming.

Lust and anger battled within Annie and lust won out as she grabbed Siobhán's hips and met Siobhán's need with her own.

"You make me crazy, Annie," Siobhán muttered against her mouth. She grabbed Annie's hand and pulled her forward. Annie barely had time to register Siobhán pushing her down onto the loveseat and dropping to her knees before she felt Siobhán's hands pushing up her dress. Her head swam from the drinks and the out-of-control lust, and Annie was too turned on to argue any more.

Siobhán yanked Annie's flimsy satin panties down and off her, then rubbed her thumb across Annie's labia. "Mmm, you are wet already. Is that for me?"

Annie moaned when Siobhán slid two fingers into her. "Always you," she managed.

"Good." Siobhán used her free hand to push Annie's leg out and to the side. She lowered her head until she was just inches from Annie's pussy. "Because I intend to make sure you never think about anyone else."

How could I? Annie thought as Siobhán buried her face between Annie's thighs and began to lick. Annie gathered Siobhán's thick hair up in her hands as Siobhán pleasured her. Annie let her head fall back, and she let out a gasping sob as her thighs tensed and she felt the first orgasm roll through her.

How could she think of *anyone* but Siobhán at a time like this?

A short while later, Annie's spinning head finally settled, and she registered the fact that she was curled up with Siobhán on the couch, and Siobhán was playing with her hair.

She looked Siobhán in the eye when she could finally form a coherent thought. "Your jealousy is completely ridiculous, you know."

Siobhán grimaced. "I know. I'm sorry."

Annie opened her mouth to argue, then realized Siobhán had agreed with her. "Really?"

"Yes." Siobhán hesitated, looking away from Annie for a moment. "Look, I—I definitely got insecure and let my jealousy get the better of me. But you're right. I was being ridiculous and sulking about something you had no control over."

Annie relaxed a little, relieved that Siobhán had at least admitted she'd been out of line. "Thank you. That makes me feel a little better."

57

"I hope you won't hold this against me," Siobhán said softly. "I'll try to rein in my jealousy in the future."

"No harm done," Annie said, trying to lighten the mood a little. She reached out and pulled Siobhán a little closer. "And I'm certainly not complaining about the orgasms."

"Kiss and make up?" Siobhán offered.

Annie sighed and pressed her lips briefly to Siobhán's. "Only if you promise to make it really, really good," she teased.

"That is definitely a promise I can keep," Siobhán said huskily.

A fter another round of sex, Siobhán tugged Annie toward the bedroom. She followed on shaky legs, feeling half-drunk and completely stupid from all the orgasms.

God, had she ever come like that? She'd lost count of them somewhere around six as one rolled straight into another. Or maybe they'd all just been part of one giant orgasm. But what did it matter? She felt so relaxed and sated she could hardly stay upright.

"Come on, *álainn*," Siobhán said, a smile in her voice. "Into bed, so."

"It's not that late," Annie said dazedly. But she let Siobhán pull her down onto the sheets and pull the blankets up over them both.

"And you can barely keep your eyes open," she murmured.

True, Annie thought as she looped an arm around Siobhán and pulled her closer.

"What does *álainn* mean?" she asked thickly. "I think I knew once, but I can't seem to remember. And I kept forgetting to ask you."

"It means beautiful. And you are, Annie. So beautiful."

Annie pressed a kiss to Siobhán's shoulder in thanks, but her eyes felt unbearably heavy, and she slipped into sleep before she could say it aloud.

A while later, Annie awoke to Siobhán staring at her with a smile on her face. "Hey," Annie said sleepily. "How long have I been out?"

"Half an hour? Forty-five minutes, maybe?" Siobhán shrugged. "Does it matter?"

"No." Annie pushed her hair out of her eyes. "Did you sleep or just lay here staring at me?"

"I was awake." Siobhán traced her fingers across Annie's cheek. "You're so beautiful when you sleep. I need to paint you sometime soon."

"Siobhán." Annie flipped onto her stomach and propped herself on her elbows. "There's something I wanted to talk to you about."

A furrow appeared over Siobhán's brow. "What about?"

"What are we doing, exactly?"

"I don't understand what you mean, Annie."

Annie wet her lips. "I'm really enjoying being with you but I … I'm not sure where this is heading. My roommate referred to you as my girlfriend, and I almost called you that earlier to the bartender, but I don't know how you feel about it. You said you couldn't stand to see someone else touch me, but I don't know what that means to you."

Siobhán smiled at her. "Does it help if I say I've been yours—and only yours—since I saw you studying my paintings at the gallery?"

"Yes." Annie swallowed past the lump in her throat. "I'm falling really hard for you," she admitted.

Siobhán pulled her in for a kiss. "Too late. I've already fallen for you." Siobhán kissed her again. "I have no intention of seeing someone else, and I hope you feel the same."

Annie smiled. "I do. I just want to be with you, Siobhán."

Chapter Seven

*R*eorganization. Temporary cutbacks. Annie stared at the reply to her email with a sick, sinking feeling. *We'll let you know when more freelance opportunities become available, but we will not be accepting new submissions in the foreseeable future.*

"Annie?" Siobhán's gentle touch on her hair made her look up from her laptop. "What is it? You look like you got horrible news."

"I did," Annie said dully. "You know how I told you that the site I regularly submit freelance stories to hadn't been posting any new submission calls lately?"

"Yes." Siobhán's brow furrowed as she took a seat beside Annie. "Did something happen?"

"They don't need me anymore. I mean, they're not saying they'll never want my work again, but they basically said they're cutting way down on the number of submission calls while they 'reorganize.' Whatever that means. They were my most reliable source of income. What the hell am I going to do?"

"Oh no!" Siobhán rubbed her arm. "I'm so sorry, Annie."

Annie leaned her head on Siobhán's shoulder. "I'm just so tired. I feel like every time I get my foot in the door somewhere and things are maybe a little better, the bottom drops out from under me. I can pick up some pieces here and there from other sites, but it won't be enough."

"I'm sorry, love." Siobhán's tone was soft and sympathetic. "Is there anything I can do?"

"Wave a magic wand and find me work?" Annie asked weakly.

"I'm afraid I can't do that. You know I would if I could though."

She did know Siobhán would help if she could, but there was little she could do besides offer sympathy. It was nice, but it didn't deposit money in her bank account or make her feel any less like a failure.

Right now, the only thing going well in her life was her relationship with Siobhán. It had been a little over a month since they'd met at the gallery and several weeks since they'd discussed exclusivity. It had been smooth sailing since the fight about Siobhán's insecurity. Annie had loved every second of the time she spent with Siobhán. Annie had even posed while Siobhán painted her a few times. Their time together seemed almost idyllic.

But the worry over her future grew worse.

If things didn't improve soon, she was just going to have to admit that she couldn't make a living with her writing and get some kind of an office job somewhere. The economy wasn't great, but Annie was pretty sure she'd be able to find something. Something that would at least pay the bills until she figured out what else to do. It was utterly and completely demoralizing. And she dreaded the thought of having to get up to go to work every day to a job that—at best—she'd tolerate and—at worst—she'd loathe. She might as well go back to journalism.

"Maybe I can help you brainstorm some new ideas," Siobhán offered, pulling her out of her melancholy thoughts. "Together, I'm sure we can come up with something."

Annie straightened and set her laptop on the ottoman beside Siobhán's. She shifted so she was facing her. "I'd welcome any help I can get. I'm doing a terrible job at it myself."

Siobhán gently grasped Annie's foot and tugged it toward her. "Come here, love. I'll rub your feet while we brainstorm."

"Okay." She moaned quietly as Siobhán began to knead her arch. "Ohhh. That feels heavenly. I'm not sure I'll be able to think while you do it."

"You just answer my questions. I'll do the thinking."

"I like the sound of that," Annie said with a small smile. The panic inside her that had begun to rise the moment she read the email was receding a little, thanks to Siobhán. Maybe they could figure out something else. Something to stave off having to apply for desk jobs a while longer. All she could do was hope.

61

"We established that you don't want to be a journalist anymore, yes?" Siobhán said, all business now.

"Yes," Annie agreed. "I can't see myself ever going back to it."

"And you love history, but you don't want to teach."

"Correct."

"But you *do* love writing."

"I do."

"Have you thought about becoming a novelist?"

Annie hesitated. "I don't feel like I have any stories in me."

Siobhán leveled her with a look as she pressed her thumb into the space between Annie's big and second toe, making them curl. "Are you saying that because you don't think you're capable of it?"

"No!" Annie protested. "Not at all. I just … I love to read, but I'm not sure a novel is what I should do. I'm not a fiction writer."

"You could write non-fiction—biographies or something."

Annie sighed, feeling frustrated. "I don't like the long format. I like shorter pieces and a more immediate connection with my readers."

"Hmm." Siobhán switched feet. "Well, that presents some dilemmas, doesn't it?"

"Unfortunately." Annie frowned. "Now you see why I'm struggling."

"I do. And it's clear that freelancing for various sites isn't working for you."

"No, not at all. I'm at the mercy of what others want. I have almost no creative control, and if they decide they don't need me, I'm out of luck." She gestured toward her laptop, indicating the email she'd gotten earlier.

Siobhán's frown deepened. "Have you thought about starting your own blog? You love writing, and the freelance posts of yours that I've read are very good. Why *not* start something of your own?"

Annie shrugged. "The thought has crossed my mind a few times. But it'll take a while to get off the ground, and even then, how would I make money?"

"Advertising, I would think."

"It just seems so daunting. Where would I begin?"

Siobhán set her foot down and patted the top of it. "Begin with something you're passionate about."

Annie laughed ruefully. "I don't even know what that is."

"Sex with me," Siobhán said with a sultry toss of her hair as she struck a vampy pose.

This time Annie's laugh was loud and long. "Yes, I do love that. But I'm not writing about lesbian sex on a blog."

"Why not? It sounds fun." But Siobhán's expression was more teasing than serious.

Annie's brief good mood evaporated. "Seriously, though, I have absolutely no idea what I'd write about."

"Well, you enjoy art. And you follow a lot of the female artists in the area. What about something to do with that?"

"You just want me to write you up and promote your work," Annie countered with a laugh.

Siobhán shrugged. "Well, I wouldn't argue if you did, but that wasn't what I intended. I just meant that it's something you're interested in, passionate about."

"I know. And that's true. Would that really be enough to fill a whole blog though?" Annie asked doubtfully.

"I'm not sure."

"And what kind of advertisers would I get? Galleries? There's only so many of those in the area, and I can't imagine they'd be that interested in a little blog like mine. Or at least not until I grew the readership."

"Well, perhaps not just artists … maybe something broader."

63

"Like what?"

"I don't know. What about a—a travel blog?"

"Hmm." Annie sighed. "A travel blog sounds amazing, but I've hardly been anywhere, except the northeast part of this country and the one semester in Ireland. I would love to travel more, but I can't afford it."

"So what about a more local focus then? Something ... something like a Boston area blog."

"What about it?" Annie asked doubtfully.

"Well, feature local attractions. Places to visit in Boston, Salem, and Cambridge. Kind of like an online travel guide for the Greater Boston area. You're great with history, you know art, you like eating out. You could spotlight a series of places, talk about tips for navigating the area, ways to save money while visiting, that sort of thing."

"That's ... yeah, that's an interesting idea," Annie said, warming to the idea. But reality reared its ugly head, and she felt like a popped balloon, rapidly deflating. "I just don't know if I'd be any good at it."

"I know it's an avenue you've never explored before, but you have the skills as a writer, you know how to research ... I really think you're suited for this."

"I guess I am pretty decent with a camera too," Annie admitted. "I had to do a lot of my own photography when I worked for the paper. Some video too."

"See?" Siobhán smiled at her. "It's coming together. What do you have to lose?"

"I'll think about it," Annie replied. "There's a ton of research I'd need to do first."

But the ideas were swirling in her head, and for the first time in a while, she felt a thrill of excitement about a potential career path.

In fact ... she looked over at Siobhán ... her life was finally coming together in a lot of ways.

Maybe things weren't quite so hopeless after all.

Two days later, when Annie got home to her own apartment, she was still thinking about Siobhán's blog idea. Siobhán seemed convinced that Annie could handle it. While Annie appreciated the faith Siobhán had in her, and loved the idea, she couldn't shake the apprehensive feeling that if she agreed to it, she'd be biting off more than she could chew.

She gave a desultory wave toward Trent, who was watching a Red Sox game on the TV. She tried not to cringe at the coffee table littered with half-empty glasses and dirty dishes.

Her thoughts quickly returned to the blog idea as she walked down the hall. She didn't like the niggling doubts she had about it, and the more she thought about it, the less plausible it seemed. What made her think that any blog she started would stand out among the millions—or maybe billions—of other blogs in the world? Thinking that was really the height of arrogance.

And while Siobhán's encouragement meant the world to her, she couldn't help but think that Siobhán was biased. Of *course*, she thought Annie would succeed. But Siobhán wasn't a writer or an editor. She was a brilliant, talented woman, but she was a studio artist, not a journalist or a blogger. What did she know?

"Ugh, I don't know why I even bother," Anne muttered under her breath as she walked toward her bedroom. "I should just accept reality and get a stupid office job like everyone else out there."

The kitchen was as messy as ever when she passed through it, and she scowled in the general direction of the living room and Trent. Great, she was going to have to clean before she could even make dinner.

Once her bags were in her room, she ventured into the kitchen, shaking her head at the piles of dishes and the faint odor of old food and musty sponges. With a sigh of resignation, she put on rubber gloves and tackled the stack of dishes.

She could scream at Trent until she was blue in the face or suck it up and clean. At the moment, cleaning seemed like less work.

She'd just finished a simple meal of scrambled eggs and toast—sans butter because Trent had "borrowed" it and forgotten to buy some to replace it for the umpteenth time—when he ambled in.

"Look, Trent, can we talk for a sec?" she asked.

"What's up, Annie?" He dropped onto one of the chairs across the table from her.

Tired and irritated by having to clean up after him, she scowled at him. "Why is it so hard for you to clean up after yourself?"

"I dunno, I just never think about it. What's the big deal?"

Annie took a deep breath. Cool and calm. Flying off the handle at him wasn't going to help anything. "The big deal is that every time I want to use the kitchen, I have to clean up after you just so I can get to anything."

"Oh, yeah. Sorry."

Trent turned to go, but the toast crumbs on her plate reminded her of another issue. "I would also appreciate it if you would replace the butter sometimes. I'm sick of trying to make toast and finding stuff I bought and paid for gone!"

"You're never here," he protested.

"And that makes it okay to take my stuff?"

"No." He looked a little sheepish. "I just don't think about it."

"I thought you were all about healthy eating anyway," she commented. "Since when are gobs of butter healthy?"

"Oh, well, there's this thing called bulletproof coffee; you put butter in it, and it's super healthy for you. It's supposed to increase alertness and performance at the gym. Plus, it's—"

"Right, got it," she cut him off. Trent was always doing some trendy diet thing. She really wasn't in the mood to sit through an infomercial about it. "But why *my* butter?"

The sheepish look deepened. "Oh, um, you get the good stuff. The organic, grass-fed fancy stuff that's so healthy for you. Regular butter doesn't work the same. Rebecca never buys any butter, and half the time, I forget to go to the store that carries it, sooo, I end up borrowing yours."

"Ooh." Annie nodded. That made sense, actually. She'd started buying the imported Irish butter after she got home from her study abroad. She'd gotten a taste for it there, and it had been her one indulgence since. "Look, I get that. Why don't you just … I don't know, give me a little extra money now and then, and I'll pick some up for you when I shop? Does that seem fair?"

Trent brightened. "Yeah, totally."

Annie sighed as she stood and carried her dishes over to the sink to wash. "And while we're at it, a 'thanks for cleaning up after me' would be really nice occasionally." She gestured toward the sparkling kitchen.

He glanced around the room as if seeing it for the first time. "Oh, wow, yeah I guess you did clean."

She scrubbed the pan she'd cooked her eggs in. *Does he really not see the mess when it's right in front of his face? Is that the problem?* She had a sudden longing for Siobhán's tidy little apartment.

"Just ... please try, Trent," she said, glancing over her shoulder. "I'm sick of feeling like I'm the only one who makes any effort around here."

"Dee cleans," he protested.

"I know she does, but she's never home. And why the hell should she clean after working and going to school? She's working herself to the bone; you're home at least twice as much as she is, and you do half the work she does around here. Not even that."

Trent frowned. "Oh, I never thought about it that way."

Annie rolled her eyes. Trent was twenty-eight years old. She couldn't believe how completely clueless he was. She'd met his mother a couple times, and it was clear she doted on him. Maybe Trent had never really grown up.

"Just ... try to think about someone other than yourself for once?" Annie said with a sigh as she put her plate in the drain board. "I'd appreciate it, and I'm sure your girlfriend would too!"

Trent nodded. Relieved that maybe she'd gotten through to him, Annie turned and headed for her bedroom.

"So is this why you're a lesbian now?" he called after her.

Annie opened her mouth to respond and then closed it. She'd thought they were making progress, but apparently not. There was no way she'd even begin to touch that statement. Not without Trent suffering bodily harm. Better to just ignore him.

She firmly closed the door to her bedroom behind her and flopped onto the bed. Without conscious thought, she reached for her phone and brought up Siobhán's number.

"Miss me already?" Siobhán asked when she answered. She sounded like she was smiling.

"I know I said I wanted to come back to my place tonight, but I think I might end up in jail for murdering my roommate," Annie blurted out in response.

"Come here then. You know I love when you spend the night."

She needed no convincing. She hopped up and packed the bags she'd so recently unpacked. Maybe she should think about leaving a few things at Siobhán's place.

Trent stopped her on the way out the door. "So, um, I was thinking about what you said earlier."

Annie raised an eyebrow at him. "Which part?"

"All of it, really." He fished in his pants' pocket for his wallet, peeling off several twenties before he handed them to her. "There, that should cover some of the back payment for butter. Sorry, that was kinda shitty of me not to think about how expensive it was when I borrowed it, ya' know?"

"I … uh, thanks, Trent. That's really nice of you," Annie said, feeling astonished as she tucked the cash into her purse.

"Oh, and um, what you said about helping around the apartment. I'll try to do more." He shuffled a little awkwardly. "I don't mean to be a douche about that either. I do cook for Dee though, you know. I prep the meals for both of us so she doesn't have to eat out all the time. The hospital food is crap." Annie stared at him, open-mouthed. "So I get why you're totally annoyed at the mess I leave, but I'm totally sick of being in the kitchen after cooking a week's worth of meals for Dee and me. I always mean to clean it up in an hour or two, and I end up putting it off."

"Oh," Annie said, flabbergasted. "I didn't realize that. I'm sorry, I didn't mean to—"

He shrugged. "Nah, you have a good point. You shouldn't have to clean up my shit just because I'm feeling lazy. How about this? I'll call the landlord

68

tomorrow about getting the dishwasher fixed. It's been broken forever, but that would make all our lives a lot easier."

It had, in fact, been broken since Annie moved in, so she rarely thought about it anymore. And since she wasn't officially on the lease—she was technically subletting from someone who had moved out a couple years ago—she'd never called the landlord herself.

"Oh, yeah, uh, that would be great," Annie stuttered. "Thanks, Trent."

"No prob. I really don't mean to piss you off, you know. So feel free to call me out when I'm being an ass. I'm just bad at paying attention to shit like that." He looked a little embarrassed. "I don't want you to hate me or anything."

Annie felt the last of her annoyance soften. "It's okay, Trent. And I didn't mean to jump down your throat about stuff. I know we're all trying to live together, and sometimes we just clash. I definitely don't hate you."

"Awesome. Glad to hear it." His expression brightened. "We cool?"

"We're cool," Annie assured him.

Forty minutes later, Annie knocked on Siobhán's door. She answered and immediately pulled Annie into her arms. "Are you okay?"

Annie chuckled. "Actually, Trent and I worked out most of our issues, and I'm feeling a lot better about things. I think we actually made some progress, and I'm hopeful the peace lasts."

"Good. But you never need to ask if you can come over," she murmured against Annie's hair. "You're always welcome here."

"Thank you." Annie smiled at her. "I know that, but I still somehow feel like I'm intruding."

"Don't be silly." Siobhán tugged her inside, then shut and locked the door after her. She turned to the little table beside the door and opened one of the drawers.

She was dressed casually in a silky, long white robe with a pattern of what looked like peonies and butterflies in rich peach, copper, and green shades. It skimmed over her curves, and Annie felt her mouth water at the sight.

BRIGHAM VAUGHN

She shifted her bag higher on her shoulder as Siobhán rummaged through the drawer. "Here." She turned back to face Annie and smiled. "Your own key. Now you can come and go as you please."

"I don't know, Siobhán," Annie said a little hesitantly. But she held out her hand and let Siobhán drop it into her palm anyway.

"You don't have to be so fecking independent, Annie!" Siobhán snapped, her dark eyes flashing. She gently folded Annie's fingers, trapping the key against her palm as she wrapped her own hand around it. She softened her tone. "You can allow someone to help you out now and again, you know?"

"I know." Annie smiled tremulously. "And I appreciate it, Siobhán, I really do."

"But you're so stubborn you'll cut your nose off to spite your face?"

"No." Annie leaned forward and pressed her lips against Siobhán's. "You're right. And I appreciate the key."

Siobhán tucked her arm into Annie's and guided her toward the bedroom. "You know what my favorite thought is?"

"Me in bed?"

Siobhán laughed. "That too. But I was thinking about coming home after a tedious meeting at the gallery and finding you reading on the couch, or typing on your laptop, or soaking in the tub. Making yourself at home here."

"That sounds really nice," Annie admitted. She dropped her bag on the floor near Siobhán's bed.

Siobhán beamed. "Then please, use the key. Surprise me one of these days."

"I'll do that," Annie agreed.

"Now what was it you were saying about being in my bed?" Siobhán asked.

Annie unknotted the tie of Siobhán's robe as she kissed her and let her actions speak for themselves.

Later that night, as Annie was drifting off to sleep, Siobhán propped herself up on one elbow. "I want to suggest something, but promise you'll listen before you dismiss it."

Annie blinked sleepily at her. "Why does that make me nervous?"

Siobhán didn't reply. Instead, she brushed Annie's hair off her face. "Earlier, I gave you the key, but what I really wanted to say was something else."

Annie felt butterflies in her stomach. "What was that?"

"Move in with me, *mo grá.*"

Annie melted a little. She'd picked up a smattering of Irish during the semester she studied there, and she knew enough to recognize that Siobhán had called her "my love." But moving in ... that was huge.

"Siobhán ... I don't know."

"I know we're moving quickly, but I love you, Annie. And you said it yourself; your roommates are insufferable half the time, and you're sick of dealing with them. Think how much nicer it would be if you lived here."

"I love you too, Siobhán," she said softly, thrilled to finally voice the words that had been hanging on the tip of her tongue for several weeks now. "But that's a huge step. I don't want to move in just because my roommate's an asshole."

Siobhán sighed. "I'm asking you to move in because I want you to be a part of my life. You're my muse, my love. You make my apartment feel like home. I want you here when I wake up in the mornings, and I want to paint to the sound of your keys clacking behind me."

"I want those things too. I'm just not sure I'm ready yet. Give me some time to think about it?" She'd rushed into relationships before only to find herself without a place to live or scrambling to find new roommates. She couldn't afford to be hasty. Her life was such a mess right now, and until she felt better about her career, she couldn't jump into something like that.

Siobhán made a face but nodded.

Annie kissed her apologetically, but Siobhán kept it brief. Rather than deepening it, she rolled over and turned out the light.

Annie stayed awake for a long while after Siobhán fell asleep, staring up at the dark ceiling while thoughts swirled through her brain.

She wanted to do what was best for both her and Siobhán, and their relationship, but she was afraid she'd just inadvertently pushed away the only person who'd been her champion in a long time. What if she'd made a mistake?

She finally fell asleep to the sound of Siobhán's even, steady breathing.

Chapter Eight

The next morning, their discussion the previous night seemed forgotten, and Annie was relieved to see that Siobhán had returned to her normal self. They fixed breakfast together and ate eggs, toast, and fresh fruit at the little table in Siobhán's kitchen while Siobhán discussed a few ideas she had for an upcoming painting.

Siobhán ate the last bite of toast and blackberry jam. "What about you?" she asked. "Have you considered the blog idea more?"

"I have, actually," Annie admitted. "And the idea is growing on me. I started to second-guess myself, but I thought more about it, and I think before I decide on anything, I'll do some research about starting a blog and make sure there isn't already one about Boston travel or attractions. See how viable an idea it is, anyway."

"Brilliant." Siobhán smiled at her. "Let me know if there's anything I can do to help."

"Thanks." Annie pushed her empty plate out of the way and gave Siobhán a brief kiss. "I appreciate that."

"Ready to get started then?"

"I am. What about you?"

Siobhán nodded. "I'm feeling the urge to paint. If I get too lost in it, remind me to come up for air occasionally, will you?"

Annie chuckled and stood. "I'll do my best."

Together, they cleared the table, washed the few dishes, and headed to the living room with fresh mugs of tea. Siobhán squirted paint onto the piece of acrylic she used as a palette and lined up a few paintbrushes on the table beside it.

BRIGHAM VAUGHN

Siobhán had finished the previous work and shown it to Annie. To Annie's astonishment, it was a painting of their first meeting, an abstract suggestion of two women standing side by side, staring at a swirl of bright colors. It was breathtaking. She couldn't wait to see it hanging in the Quinn gallery at Siobhán's next show.

"I love the possibilities a fresh canvas offers," Siobhán said with a happy sigh.

"Ugh, I'm the opposite," Annie admitted. "Well, I find blank Word documents intimidating anyway. Sometimes, I'll just type some gibberish so I don't see all the blank, white space mocking me."

"Oh, sometimes if my creativity is running low, I'll just slap paint on a canvas with no idea what direction I'm going. It can help jumpstart things." She peered around the canvas at Annie who was setting up her laptop across the room. Siobhán beamed at her. "But I don't have to worry about that with you around, do I?"

Annie rolled her eyes. "You aren't really serious about that, are you?"

"About you inspiring me? Of course, I am, Annie. I mean every word of it. My feelings for you bubble up, and it spills out onto my canvas. Our relationship feeds my creativity. You saw the last piece I did; how can you doubt that?"

Flabbergasted, all Annie could do was stare at her for a moment. "You really mean it then? Calling me your muse?"

"Of course, I do." Siobhán stood and crossed the room to her "I meant every word of it. You make me feel so gloriously alive and creative, Annie. Like nothing can stop me."

Annie swallowed hard. "You make me feel that way too. I was so dull and dead for a while, and you blew my life wide open. To think, if I hadn't gone to the gallery that night ..."

Siobhán cupped Annie's cheek in her hand. "But you did." She kissed Annie sweetly with all the pent up passion she seemed to carry with her all the time.

Annie let out a gasp and kissed her back, thanking her lucky stars she'd met Siobhán that night. If she hadn't, her life would have continued on down that dull path she'd been treading. Siobhán's arrival had sent her tumbling off course into a new and exciting direction.

74

Siobhán pulled back with a reluctant sounding sigh. "I suppose we should work. I'd rather tear your clothes off and make you come though."

"Trust me, I'd rather do that too," Annie said with a wry smile. "But I suppose we'll have to be a little more disciplined since neither of us have nine to five jobs to go off to every day. Or we'll get nothing done but each other."

"That sounds much nicer to me," Siobhán muttered, but she blew Annie a little kiss as she crossed the room to her easel.

"I wouldn't be much of a muse if I let you slack off," Annie pointed out as she dragged her computer onto her lap. She liked working with Siobhán like this. Both of them in the same room, focused on their own projects.

"I'm not sure I wanted one that was such a taskmaster," Siobhán teased. "But I suppose you're right."

They were both silent for a while as Annie began her work.

She searched for Boston area blogs and came up with an extensive list. She skimmed through the descriptions, finding that most were parenting blogs or design and foodie blogs. A couple were music blogs, and one had local news. She even found a few specifically about art. But the ones that seemed to have more of a travel or event theme were old and hadn't been updated in a year or two.

It seemed that Siobhán's idea was feasible at least. That was something. It sent a burst of energy through Annie, and she decided her next step should probably be to make a list of places in Boston to feature on the blog. Maybe a few she'd been to before and might only need to stop by long enough to get some decent photos. She could sprinkle in a few new places too. She could also do a list of attractions accessible via public transportation, which would be a big draw for people like Annie and Siobhán who didn't own a car. Maybe she could also do a series of posts about free attractions in Boston.

She lit up at the thought. It would help keep her budget low, give her a regular post idea, *and* attract plenty of readers. *This free series is going to be so great!* she thought, feeling excited and eager to tackle the project.

Siobhán's suggestion about the blog had really been fantastic. Annie knew it would take a while before she got the kind of blog traffic she'd need in order to attract sponsors, but she was sure she could do it. Siobhán's belief in her had given her flagging confidence a major boost.

Her fingers flew over the keyboard as she typed the list of free attractions, then created a second list for inexpensive destinations in the Boston area.

I should probably check to be sure no one's already done that, Annie thought, her excitement dimming a little. *Oh well, if they have, I'll have to find an angle no one has ever done before. I'm sure I can come up with something,* she reasoned. No need to assume the worst about every small bump that came along.

A quick search revealed there were a few lists on websites, but nothing as comprehensive as she was planning, so she made notes and created a rough outline of what she needed to do next. Things were beginning to come together, and she sat back and stretched with a little sigh of satisfaction. A glance at the clock showed her that she'd been working for a little over an hour.

Oh, I should do a list of lesser-known Boston-area attractions as well, she thought. *Let's see, there's the Museum of Bad Art in Brookline, the Cambridge Center Roof Garden in Kendall Square, the park at the top of Corey Hill, the gondola rides on the Charles River—now that would be a fun date with Siobhán—oh, and the Boston Tango Society's free lessons on the Weeks Footbridge … Can't forget that. Plus, the skinniest house in the United States. That should go on the list too.*

There were so many things Annie had always wanted to try, and she'd never had a partner she felt like she could do them with. It seemed like in so many relationships, her partners had been content to stay in and do nothing.

She loved the moments like this one—quiet moments where she and Siobhán both worked—but she didn't want to spend half her life sitting on the couch being bored.

Annie watched Siobhán paint for a few moments, her skin dappled gold in the sunlight streaming in the window as she swished the paintbrush over the canvas with sure strokes. Annie was pretty sure she'd never get bored with Siobhán.

Siobhán was an interesting, dynamic person, and she'd awoken the person Annie had been before a failed career and a string of dull relationships had put her to sleep. Annie couldn't blame her previous partners for that—it was all on her—but it was a reminder that she could be whomever she wanted to be. And she liked the person she was becoming.

Siobhán pushed her hair off her face with the back of her forearm, leaving a little smear of green paint on her cheek. Annie smiled at the sight. God, she loved Siobhán. The talk they'd had earlier about Annie's career had relieved some of her anxiety about the future, and it made Annie wonder if she'd been holding back with Siobhán too much. What if there was a way she could show Siobhán how much she meant to her? Some gesture to reassure her that Annie was definitely on the same page, even if she wasn't quite ready to take the leap and move in together.

Giving Siobhán a key to her apartment seemed like a rather hollow gesture since Siobhán had never even been to her place. And they weren't at a point where they were ready to list each other as emergency contacts yet.

Annie wracked her brain for ideas, and it wasn't until she thought about what she'd done in previous relationships that the idea came to her. "Would you want to meet my parents?" Annie blurted out.

Siobhán looked up from her canvas. "Your parents?"

Annie nodded. "They live just outside Boston in Concord. I was thinking we could meet them for lunch sometime soon. "

"Oh. Yes, of course, Annie. If you're ready for that." Siobhán gave her a quizzical look, as if surprised by Annie's suggestion.

"Yes. I'm sorry if you feel like I've been holding back. I don't mean to," Annie said apologetically.

"No, I understand. I'm sorry if I'm too pushy sometimes." Siobhán looked abashed. "I don't mean to do that either. I'm just so happy to be with you, and I want it all. Now."

"I know," Annie said softly. "And I love your enthusiasm, Siobhán. I just have to be sure I'm not putting myself in a bad place. The last time I moved in with someone, I was left with almost nothing when we split. I'd gotten rid of my things because Mark's were nicer, and I ended up with no apartment and almost no furniture. That's why I ended up living with Rebecca, Trent, and Dee." Annie made a face. "And I don't want to have a repeat of that. My roommates can definitely be a pain but ..."

"No, I get that, Annie. I really am sorry I pushed. You move in when you feel ready. I promise I'm not going anywhere. Just know you're always welcome here."

"I appreciate that. I just have to get my life in order first."

"Promise you'll tell me what I can do to help," Siobhán said. "Please don't be too independent to do that."

"I can agree to that." A thought had been niggling inside Annie's brain since she started planning the blog. She'd been a little hesitant to ask Siobhán, but she decided to bite the bullet and blurt it out. "Actually, there *is* something I thought of. And it involves your paintings."

Siobhán's eyes lit up. She reached out and set her brush on the palette. "Oooh. What is it?"

"It seems like the blog is going to be a viable idea, so I wondered if you would be willing to paint a banner image for me. I looked through some stock photo sites, and there are plenty of images of the Boston skyline but none of them really excite me. I thought maybe you could paint something instead. Like a stylized version of the city skyline, familiar, but something fresh and new that no one else would have."

"Oh! Yes, I love that idea!" Siobhán seemed to glow with excitement, and the last of Annie's nerves about asking her for the favor vanished. "It's *brilliant*."

Annie shared a smile with her. "I hoped you'd think so."

"We could turn them into icons for your other social media and use the design on business cards too. Really tie everything together with a solid theme."

Annie smiled at Siobhán's use of the word "we." She liked the idea of this being a collaborative effort with Siobhán. "I love that."

"How soon would you need it?"

"Oh, not for a little while. I'm going to write a number of blog posts ahead of time so I have a solid amount of content right off the bat."

"That sounds like a good idea."

"We'll probably need to go out a fair amount for a while so I can get material," Annie pointed out.

Siobhán snorted. "Oh dear, I'll have to take my beautiful girlfriend out and enjoy the town. What a sacrifice!"

Annie laughed. "I know it seems like fun, but I'll have to take notes and photos. I *will* be working."

"Oh, that's fine. I don't mind. One of these days, I'll take you on a walking tour of Boston while I take photos of everything I think I might ever paint."

"Sounds fair." Annie shared a smile with Siobhán. "Hopefully, the research will benefit both of our professional lives."

"I like the thought of that. Do you have any ideas for the blog design or colors or anything?"

"I don't. Should I pick something out now?"

Siobhán hummed thoughtfully for a moment, then nodded. "I think so. There are a limited number of themes available, I'd imagine, and I can always choose my palette based on whatever you pick. It'll probably be easier if we start with that instead of doing it the other way 'round."

"This is really coming together," she said happily.

Siobhán gave her a tender smile. "I love how happy you look when you talk about it."

"I'm excited about this," she admitted. "I can't remember the last time I felt that way about something for my career."

Siobhán beamed. "How about this? I'll finish up this piece I'm working on currently, and as soon as you have the colors picked, we'll talk about your ideas for the design of the banner. I need to know exactly what you have in mind. And as soon as it's painted, we can take it to the Quinn gallery and get it photographed with Gabriel's equipment. It'll be high-resolution for your blog, the same quality as what he puts on the gallery website. I'll have to run it by him, but I'm sure he'll say yes."

"Oh! That's great," Annie said, Siobhán's enthusiasm spilling over onto her. "I was just going to use my camera."

"No, this'll be better. And maybe we can figure out a way to showcase the work in the gallery and direct people to your blog once it's up and running. I'm sure I can get Gabriel to work with me. Especially since you're an old friend of his."

"You'd do that for me?" Annie asked.

Siobhán gave her a bewildered look. "Of course, I would, Annie. I love you. Why wouldn't I do whatever I could to help you succeed?"

Annie glanced down. "Because no one's ever done that for me before," she said softly.

"Well, I'm not anyone."

That was true. Siobhán was unlike anyone Annie had ever known.

"**A**nnie?"

She looked up from her laptop at Siobhán. "Yes?"

Siobhán had been painting all morning, and Annie had been immersed in her own work on the blog.

"I've finished the painting I've been working on."

"That was quick," Annie said, surprised. It had been less than a week since their conversation about Siobhán painting an image for her blog. She'd expected to have a few more days to choose a blog theme, but it appeared Siobhán was already done with the previous work.

"I know." Siobhán smiled at her and stood. Her baggy black T-shirt draped down one arm and she had a smear of green paint across it, like she'd reached up to itch her shoulder. "Would you like to see?"

"I'd love to." She set her laptop aside and walked over to the canvas.

Annie gasped when she saw it. It was a gorgeous, semi-abstract rendering of Boston Common. The colors were vivid and drew the eye around the painting. Tucked in between two trees were figures walking hand-in-hand. The bright swirls of colors radiated out from them and filled the air.

"You're memorializing our relationship," she said softly.

Siobhán nodded. "This collection is heading in a different direction than I expected." She reached out and skimmed a hand along Annie's arm. "I love where you're taking me though."

Annie turned and kissed her. She didn't have words to express how much she loved Siobhán's art. Or Siobhán herself.

80

Siobhán drew back and smiled up at her.

"It's incredible," Annie finally managed. She frowned when a thought occurred to her. "Does this mean you need me to make a decision on the blog theme? I'm still dithering."

"It can wait a few days if you're not ready," Siobhán said. "Or I can help you pick. Whichever you'd prefer."

Annie mulled it over. "Give me another day or two to think about it. If I can't make a decision, I'll have you help."

"Sounds good."

"Oh, that's not putting you behind though, is it?" Annie asked.

"No. I can work on some smaller project in the meantime. Actually, I know you're busy, but can you take a break?" Siobhán asked. "Maybe half an hour or something."

"Sure. Do you want to make lunch or something?"

Siobhán shook her head. "Later. Right now, I want to paint you."

"What did you have in mind?" Annie asked. It was one thing to know Siobhán had included her in a painting; it was another to pose for the painting and know she was the focus.

"You nude. In our bed."

Annie smiled at Siobhán referring to it as their bed. Truthfully, Siobhán's place was feeling more and more like home lately.

"Okay," she agreed. "Just tell me what to do."

Twenty minutes later, Annie was stretched out in a tangle of white sheets, and Siobhán peered at her from behind the easel.

"Slide your left leg a little farther to the left."

Annie raised an eyebrow at Siobhán. "How far?"

She chuckled. "Not enough to see anything between those gorgeous legs. Just enough so there's a shadow to hint at it."

81

Annie parted her legs a little farther.

"Perfect! Now, you're going to need to lie very still. Are you comfortable enough to hold that for half an hour or so? You'll be able to shift a little if you need to, but I need you to remain in that pose."

Annie took stock of her body. One leg was drawn up—her foot flat on the bed—but a pillow tucked against her thigh helped support it. She was quite comfortable at the moment, actually. "Yeah, I should be fine like this for quite a while."

"If you need to move, warn me."

"Okay."

"And if you need to sneeze, try to avoid it."

"I will," Annie agreed, laughing.

Siobhán grew quiet, and Annie heard the rough sketch of pencil on paper. Siobhán had told her she'd sketch the scene first, then fill in with color later, so Annie would have to hold the pose for a shorter time.

"I actually thought about doing some modeling for the art students in the classes at school when they did life drawing," Annie said after a while. She could lay there without moving, but she wasn't sure she could do it without talking at all.

Siobhán peered around the corner of the canvas at her. "You didn't though?"

"Nah. I chickened out."

"You would have been stunning," Siobhán said. "But I'm not entirely sorry you'll be my model exclusively."

"How do you know?" Annie joked. She had been a little apprehensive at first, but she began to enjoy the feeling of Siobhán's gaze on her body and the whisper of a breeze. It made her skin pebble with goosebumps and her nipples harden. "Maybe I'll take it up now that I'm comfortable with it."

"If I believed you, I might be struggling with my jealousy right now," Siobhán said teasingly.

Annie smiled. Siobhán was right. She enjoyed this, but she couldn't imagine posing so intimately for anyone else.

Siobhán groaned. "How am I supposed to focus on my work when you look like that?"

Annie chuckled. "You can have your way with me after."

"Not to worry, *álainn*, I will." Siobhán shot her a smoldering glance from behind the painting. "Believe me; I will."

Chapter Nine
August

They sat at a table at a seafood restaurant in the North End—not far from Annie's place—as they waited for her parents to meet them. She felt like her stomach was twisted in knots. Siobhán rested her hand on Annie's to still her drumming fingers. "Are you really that nervous?"

Annie glanced up from the white linen tablecloth she'd been staring blankly at and nodded. "Sorry, I'm stressed out about seeing my family," she admitted.

"I thought you got along with them." Siobhán sounded mystified.

"I *do*, or at least, I do most of the time. Sometimes, my mom can be a bit hard on me, is all. I'm just nervous because it's been a long time since I've had them meet someone, and I want it to go well."

A frown flickered across Siobhán's face. "Are you worried they won't like me?"

"No, of course not," Annie protested with a laugh. "How could anyone not love you? You're incredible. I'm just being ridiculous. I'm sure it'll go fine." She glanced toward the entrance and caught a glimpse of her parents approaching the table. "And here they are." She stood and Siobhán followed suit.

"Hi, Mom." Annie greeted her mother with a kiss on the cheek.

Heather Slocum was tall and slim with blonde hair expertly dyed to blend away the gray and cool blue eyes. At the moment, she wore a natural linen sheath dress and nude pumps that elongated her already long legs. She always looked stylish and put together. Physically, Annie looked a lot like her mother, but she had never quite managed to live up to her mother's effortless fashion sense.

84

Siobhán had assured Annie she looked wonderful in the cobalt blue wrap dress she'd dug out of the back of her closet and accessorized with a few borrowed pieces from Siobhán's wardrobe, but Annie knew it didn't hold a candle to the white maxi dress Siobhán wore. Annie would have felt frumpy in it, but Siobhán looked like a goddess.

"Hi, Pumpkin," her dad said with a twinkle in his eye. "You're looking wonderful." Annie hugged him tightly. James Slocum was a big, burly guy with reddish blond hair, blue eyes, and a gruff but warm demeanor.

"Thanks, Dad." She glanced over at her mother. "Mom, Dad, this is Siobhán Murray. My girlfriend."

Siobhán offered them both a wide smile. "It's lovely to meet you, Mr. and Mrs. Slocum."

"Heather, please." Her mother smiled, but it wasn't overly warm as she took Siobhán's hand.

"And James." Her father's eyes crinkled at the corners as he heartily shook Siobhán's hand. "Before I forget to say it, both of you ladies look beautiful today."

"Thank you, James." Siobhán shot him a dazzling smile. "That's very kind of you."

Her mother leaned in for a kiss on the cheek, then gave Annie a critical once over. "Have you gained weight?" she said with a frown. "You know how important exercise is now that you're over thirty. You need to take care of yourself."

Siobhán shot her a glance out of the corner of her eye when Annie gritted her teeth together and chose to ignore her mother's comment. She *had* been slacking lately, but she hadn't put on more than five pounds. Certainly nothing to be concerned about.

"Why don't you have a seat," Annie said in a falsely cheerful tone. "I told them two more people were coming, and the hostess said they'd send a waiter around when you arrived."

Her parents took seats across from them at the table, and Annie scrambled for ideas to get the conversation started. Her father saved her.

"So, you're from Ireland, Siobhán?" James tripped over the pronunciation a little, but managed to get somewhere near it.

85

"I am." Siobhán offered him a bright smile. "I grew up in a town called Bray. It's on the coast of the Irish sea, just a bit south of Dublin."

Heather glanced back and forth between them. "So did you two meet while Annie was studying there?"

"Oh, no," Siobhán said with a laugh. "That would have been an interesting coincidence, but if I remember right from what Annie's said, I was moving to Boston somewhere around the time she was visiting Ireland."

"So where did you meet?"

"At an art gallery," Annie explained. "Earlier this summer, Siobhán had a show at the gallery I go to semi-regularly, and we struck up a conversation." She smiled over at Siobhán. "And I fell head-over-heels."

Siobhán reached out and squeezed her hand.

"You're an artist then?" James asked.

"I am. A painter," Siobhán explained. "Mainly acrylics, but I've done some mixed media, and I dabbled with oil pastels for a while.

Heather frowned. "Have you had much luck with your art?"

"Quite a bit, actually," Siobhán said with a smile. "I've had three very successful shows at the Quinn gallery and was recently approached by a couple looking to commission a piece."

"How interesting." Heather turned to Annie. "Quinn? Didn't you have a friend with that name?

"Yes. The same Quinn, actually. Gabriel dated my roommate Sylvia."

"Oh, yes, I remember her. Lovely girl."

Annie suppressed a grin. If only her mother knew what she'd gotten up to with Sylvia. And Gabriel, for that matter. But she wasn't about to bring *that* up at dinner.

"I stayed in contact with Gabriel and occasionally visit his gallery," Annie explained.

"I'm quite grateful to Gabriel Quinn," Siobhán said with a smile. "Without him, I wouldn't have met Annie."

James gave her a broad smile. "I came prepared with a 'don't you dare hurt my daughter' speech, but I can see I won't have to give that today!"

Annie chuckled. "I made you promise not to harass Siobhán too much, Dad!"

"And I won't. I clearly don't need to." He beamed at them both.

"Will you be meeting with Siobhán's parents sometime in the near future?" Heather asked.

When Siobhán didn't answer immediately, Annie glanced over at her and saw a tight smile on her face. It occurred to her that she had no idea what Siobhán's parents were like. She'd mentioned an uncle, but next to nothing about her parents. Odd.

"Well, I hardly think we'll be taking a trip to Ireland anytime soon," Annie said lightly. "Although you know I loved it when I was there. I certainly wouldn't mind visiting again!"

"You should have seen how many photos Annie took while she was there," James joked. "She even took photos of the pigeons!"

Annie laughed. "I did, but they were *Irish* pigeons. They seemed more thrilling than the ones we have in Boston. But I suppose that's just because I was excited about traveling and being on my own for the first time."

Her mother shook her head. "I spent that whole semester worrying something terrible would happen. It hadn't been so long since there had been bombings in Ireland."

A shadow crossed Siobhán's face. "When exactly were you there, Annie?"

"Hmm, it must have been the spring semester of 2001," Annie said.

"The ceasefire was 1998, and everyone was very relieved," Siobhán said softly.

"Oh, I suppose you must have grown up in the midst of that conflict, didn't you?" Heather took a sip of her water.

Siobhán shrugged. "While I knew it was going on and was horrified by the fighting, it had little impact on my life. The bombings were mostly in the North. There were none in the Republic while I was growing up. County Wicklow was very safe. My father never liked me going into Dublin with friends, and he wasn't happy I went to university there after my secondary education was done, but it was just garden-variety worries that any parent has about their child in a big city. His worries had nothing to do with the IRA."

"Oh, I had similar worries about Annie living in Boston," James said. "But that's interesting to know. I guess we assumed that the conflict spilled into everyone's life there."

Heather cleared her throat. "I'm sorry I brought up such a sensitive topic."

Siobhán shrugged. "It's an unavoidable part of Ireland's history, I'm afraid. I'd love to pretend we're all green rolling fields, sheep, and whiskey distilleries, but as Annie and I have talked about, there's a dark side to the country too."

"Well, it's not one we need to discuss on such a lovely day." Heather's smile looked pasted-on. "Now, where is the waiter? I'd like to order a drink."

Siobhán shot Annie a look, and Annie offered her a helpless shrug. Her mother had never liked conflict and was always trying to smooth things over in favor of pleasantness. Although that never stopped her from the occasional needle-y comments she made about Annie's appearance. And career. Annie knew her mother cared, but she wished she would go about it differently.

Heather waved to catch the attention of a nearby waiter. He came over promptly. "I'm sorry. Have you been helped?"

"We have not," Heather said crisply.

"I'm very sorry about that. Let me get your drink and appetizer orders in right away."

They all ordered wine, except for her father who got a beer, and then agreed to share a few appetizers. Annie was finally able to relax a fraction, and she reached out to grab Siobhán's thigh under the tablecloth. Siobhán gave her a soft smile in return.

The rest of the lunch passed more easily. She was polite, but it never really seemed like her mother warmed up to Siobhán. Annie couldn't figure out why, either. Siobhán was beautiful, successful, and she made Annie happy. What more could her mom want?

By the time their lunch wrapped up and her father asked for the bill, Annie felt like she needed to talk to her mother about it.

"I'm going to use the restroom before we leave," Annie said. "Mom, would you like to come with me?"

Her mother looked surprised. "I suppose."

Annie kept her thoughts to herself until they reached the privacy of the women's restroom. Thankfully, the only occupant was leaving as they walked in, and the moment they were alone, Annie turned to her. "Why are you being so cool with Siobhán? Do you have a problem with her?"

Heather sighed. "Of course we don't have a problem with her. Siobhán is lovely, dear."

"Then why are you acting like she doesn't belong? I care about her, and I want her to feel like she's welcome around our family."

"I understand she's someone you enjoy spending time with, but surely, it's not as serious as you imply."

Annie bit back a sigh. "It's serious enough that I'm considering moving in with her."

Her mother's lips flattened into a thin line. "I'm not sure that's wise, Annie."

"And why not?"

"You need to think of your long-term future. You're not getting any younger, and if you want children someday ... well, you need to stop experimenting and settle down."

"Experimenting?" Annie blinked at her. "I'm not *experimenting* with Siobhán. And what makes you think I couldn't have children with Siobhán if we chose to? Do you have something against two women raising children together?"

"Oh, don't be ridiculous." Her mother laughed lightly. "You know your father and I are fine with lesbians. Sherry and Dana are a lovely couple and their children are delightful."

Sherry and Dana were her parents' neighbors. "But that's suddenly not okay for *me*?" Annie asked, unbelievably hurt by her mother's treatment of her and Siobhán. She'd never known her mother to be a bigot, so this came as a complete shock.

She sighed heavily as if annoyed that Annie was making such a big deal about it. "You have these whims, Annie. You flit from one thing to another. You think you know what you want, but you'll change your mind. This is no different than your desire to be a journalist. We know how long that lasted."

Annie forced herself to take a deep breath. "I admit I screwed up there. I thought I knew what I wanted to do with my career. But that was over ten years ago! I've grown up, and I think I have a better idea of what I want now."

"I don't see you pursuing any other serious fields," her mother said. "Unless you have a new career you haven't told us about."

"Actually," Annie said coldly, "I do. I'm starting my own website about travel to Boston. It will be … an online guidebook for the area." She didn't dare use the word blog. She could imagine the reaction that would cause.

Her mother chuckled. "Oh, do be serious, Annie. That's hardly a *career*. And with you dating a lesbian artist? Being a struggling couple together no doubt sounds romantic, but it won't last. You'll grow tired of it once the luster wears off, and you'll want someone more financially stable."

"Siobhán is quite successful, you know," Annie pointed out. "She's hardly struggling, and I really think I can make this Boston travel guide a success myself."

"Well, you know I wish you luck; I'm just skeptical. And remember you can't take too long to make up your mind about what you want or all the good men will be gone." Her face brightened. "Oh, did I tell you? Gloria's son is a doctor and recently divorced. Would you like me to set you up with him?"

"No, I would not," Annie said through gritted teeth. "I happen to be in a serious relationship with someone already. We aren't seeing other people. And I'm very happy." She stalked out of the bathroom and nearly bowled over a woman attempting to come in. "Sorry," she muttered.

Siobhán sat chatting amicably with her father when she reached the table, but one look at Annie made her straighten, a worried frown creasing her face.

"Where's your mother?" James asked with an equally concerned expression on his face. Siobhán gave Annie a questioning look that Annie couldn't begin to respond to at the moment.

"We had a difference of opinion," Annie said stiffly. She bent down and kissed his cheek. "I'll talk to you soon, Dad. Siobhán, let's go. Please."

Siobhán looked startled, but she stood and allowed Annie to take her hand. Annie hurried out of the restaurant, cheeks burning with color as she tried to fight back tears.

"What on earth happened, Annie?" Siobhán said.

"Can we go back to my place please?" Annie said, her voice tight and strained. "I really don't want to cry in the middle of Hanover Street."

Chapter Ten

"I can't believe them!" Annie snarled as she unlocked the door to her apartment. She wasn't quite sure why she'd headed there instead of to Siobhán's place, except for the fact that it was closer. "Well, *her.*" Her tears had quickly turned to anger.

Siobhán gave her a perplexed frown. "I'm still not sure I understand what happened, Annie."

"My *mother*," she spat, "is convinced my bisexuality is a *phase.* According to her, I'm just 'experimenting' with you. I should be settling down with a man and making babies. And getting a serious career. Apparently, the things I *actually* want aren't good enough."

"I'm so sorry, *mo grá,*" Siobhán said softly. "That was unfair of her."

"Unfair?" Tears sprang to Annie's eyes, and she fumbled to remove her shoes. "It's ridiculous. I always thought my parents were supportive. Turns out, I was wrong."

"Your father was lovely." Siobhán's tone was placating. She was right, but Annie wasn't in the mood to be soothed.

"Good. Maybe I won't have to yell at him." Annie grabbed her heels and stalked toward her bedroom, Siobhán trailing after.

She stripped out of her clothes, tossing them on the little chair near her makeshift desk. "I'm just fed up with it. Why is it that people think our relationship is somehow less valid just because I've dated a man before?" she ranted.

"Annie." Siobhán reached for her, but Annie pulled away. "It doesn't matter."

"Of *course,* it matters!" she exploded.

92

"Hear me out, Annie. Yes, it matters to you, but it doesn't matter in our relationship." She frowned. "Unless ... Do you not want to be with me? Does what your mother thinks matter more than ... than us?"

"What?" The words stopped Annie in her tracks, and she turned back to face Siobhán.

Siobhán took her hands and looked her in the eye. "Does this change how you feel about me, Annie?"

"No! Of course not! Why would it possibly matter if my mother ..." It occurred to her that Siobhán had probably had a similar conversation with Laura at some point. And Laura had picked her family. "Oh, God, Siobhán. No. Don't think that! I want to be with you. My mother can fuck off," Annie said grimly. "I'm not giving you up for anything. Much less her."

Siobhán gave her a tremulous smile. "I'm sorry I doubted you, Annie, I just ..."

"No, I'm sorry," Annie said. "Come here." She drew Siobhán close and brushed their lips together. Siobhán relaxed against her, softening, and Annie deepened the kiss. She needed to show Siobhán exactly how much she meant to her. "I love you, Siobhán," she murmured between kisses. "I've been so happy since I've met you, and I love being with you. I'm not going anywhere, I promise."

Siobhán shuddered a little in her arms, and Annie's heart ached when she caught a glimpse of Siobhán's face. She didn't know what else to say to reassure Siobhán how important she was to her. Maybe if she showed her physically, she'd understand.

"Sit down," she coaxed. "Let me show you how much you mean to me." Annie gently pushed her to the bed and knelt in front of her. She pushed Siobhán's skirt higher on her thighs and eased her panties down and off.

Siobhán shivered when Annie ran her hands up Siobhán's strong, lean legs. Annie pressed a kiss to her calf, then trailed her lips upward, lingering on her knee for a moment before she traversed the soft, pale skin of her thigh.

Siobhán's skirt fluttered over her head as Annie moved higher, and she was engulfed in the heady rich musk of Siobhán's body. She settled Siobhán's thighs on her shoulders and breathed in deep. Light filtered through the thin fabric, dimming Annie's view of Siobhán's most intimate parts, but by now,

Annie knew them well. She reached out and ran the backs of her fingers across the flesh between Siobhán's legs and heard a quiet gasp.

Unable to wait any longer, Annie leaned in, pressing a kiss to the smooth swell of Siobhán's lips. She tasted Siobhán's juices on her mouth and lapped at her softly, chasing the flavor of her arousal to the source.

Siobhán let out a throaty moan, and Annie had a fleeting thought about her roommates overhearing before she decided she didn't care. She used her fingers to part Siobhán's folds and licked her way upward. Siobhán shuddered when she hit her clit, and Annie reached around to grasp her hip as she buried her face in Siobhán's pussy and licked harder.

"Annie," Siobhán keened. "*Please.*"

Annie gently slid two fingers into Siobhán's wetness, then swirled her tongue around Siobhán clit. She continued in a relentless rhythm until Siobhán shattered, her hands gripping Annie's head to hold her in place, and she cried out softly.

After a moment, Siobhán let go of her with a soft "oh," and Annie emerged from under her skirt, discreetly wiping her face.

Siobhán gave her a dazed look as she settled onto her back. "Oh, Annie."

Annie grinned and curled up on the bed beside her.

"You're very convincing, *álainn,*" she said with a sigh.

Laughing and relieved that Siobhán seemed more like her usual self, Annie curled around her. "I'm glad to hear it."

Siobhán let her head fall to the side. She reached up to touch Annie's face with her fingertips, drawing them gently across her cheeks. "I'm sorry I doubted you. I ..." A pained expression crossed her face, and she didn't continue.

"It's okay," Annie said softly. "You don't have to talk about it now, if you don't want."

"Thank you." Siobhán drew her in for a kiss, and when she pulled back, she was smiling faintly. "You know, I can taste myself on your mouth. It's delicious, but I think I'd rather taste you."

Annie grinned at her, allowing her to change the subject. For now. "I'm not stopping you."

Siobhán sat up and stripped out of her dress, tossing it—along with her bra and panties—to the floor. Annie had already taken off her dress, but she got fully naked and watched Siobhán.

The bounce of her breasts was mesmerizing.

Siobhán ran her hand up Annie's leg. "Where should I start? With those tight little nipples?"

They had tightened into hard aching nubs. "That seems like a good place," she said breathlessly.

Siobhán walked forward on her hands and knees and lowered her mouth to Annie's breasts. She avoided the nipples at first, focusing instead on the inner curve. She licked and nipped at the flesh there until Annie squirmed and coaxed her toward the sensitive peaks. Siobhán hummed as she drew one into her mouth, and Annie let out a needy sigh. Siobhán suckled and gently teased it with her teeth until Annie couldn't stand it.

"The other one," she said with a quiet gasp, urging her toward it. Siobhán's long hair dragged across her sensitive skin as she moved to Annie's left breast and repeated the teasing. She switched back to the right, then moved from one to the other until Annie could hardly think straight.

Annie shuddered as Siobhán trailed a hand over her stomach and between her legs. She softly fingered Annie's wet folds, urging her toward the edge of a climax she couldn't quite reach. It was incredible, but Annie needed more.

"Oh God, I ..." She couldn't even get the words out.

"Tell me what you need," Siobhán coaxed.

Annie reached out blindly, yanked open the nightstand drawer, and rummaged in it until her fingers closed on her favorite vibrator. "Here," she said as she thrust it toward Siobhán, praying she'd remembered to charge it recently. Siobhán's eyes lit up.

It took Siobhán a moment to figure out the controls, but she gave Annie a wicked grin when it began to buzz in her hand. She leaned forward, propping herself up on one hand as she straddled Annie. "Inside or out," she asked, leaning down to kiss Annie before she could answer. "Tell me what you like best."

"Outside," Annie said with a gasp when Siobhán drew back. "Mostly on my clit."

"Outside it is, so."

Annie jerked when Siobhán brought the buzzing toy in contact with her lips, but she moaned when Siobhán used it to gently part them and passed it over her clit, the barest whisper of a sensation.

"Light like that?"

"Yes," Annie said with a gasp. She began to move her hips in time with Siobhán's passes over the most sensitive spot on her body, but she wasn't sure if she was running from the contact or seeking more. She just knew she felt helpless under Siobhán's touch.

Siobhán sat back and gently pushed Annie's knees up. Annie let them fall open, giving Siobhán better access to her.

The look in Siobhán's eyes as she brought the buzzing toy to Annie's clit again made the tension in her ramp even higher, and she shuddered at the contact. It didn't take long before her hips were rising and falling with the rhythm of Siobhán's movements, and Annie felt herself nearing the edge again.

When Siobhán slid two fingers into her, Annie brought the pillow to her face to muffle her cries. And when Siobhán pressed the vibrator firmly to Annie's clit, she came apart, screaming into the fabric as her whole body shuddered.

Everything went blank for a moment as she rode the waves of the orgasm, mindless to anything but the pleasure streaking through her body. When she finally, dazedly, returned to earth, she weakly pushed the pillow away, then Siobhán's hand. "Too sensitive," she said with a gasp. "Holy shit."

Siobhán turned off the vibrator and tossed it onto the bed next to them, grinning at her.

Annie reached out and drew Siobhán down alongside her.

"If I'd known how much you liked vibrators, I would have suggested you bring one to my place immediately," Siobhán teased. She pressed a kiss to Annie's cheek.

"That can be arranged in the future," Annie said with a soft laugh. "And trust me; it's not just the vibrator. I don't come that hard when I get myself off."

"Now there's a pretty picture." Siobhán propped herself up on one hand.

"What's that?"

"Watching you use the toy to pleasure yourself. I think I'd like to see that."

"That can be arranged too." They shared a grin. "What if I asked you to do the same?"

Siobhán ran her fingertips down Annie's stomach and trailed her fingers through the soft bit of hair at the apex of her thighs. "I'd say you had a date," she said huskily.

Annie flipped onto her side, bringing the front of her body in line with Siobhán's. In the process, Siobhán's hand was dislodged, and she brought it to Annie's hip.

"Thank you for meeting my family today," Annie said softly. "Even if it didn't go quite how we planned."

"You're welcome. I'm only sorry about my reaction when we got back here." A shadow passed across Siobhán's face. "I care about you so much, Annie, and it scares me to think of losing you."

"You aren't going to lose me, Siobhán," Annie reassured her. "Especially not because of my parents."

The sound of Siobhán swallowing was audible in the otherwise silent room. "Are you sure?"

Annie nodded. "I'm sure. Can I ask you something though?"

"Sure." Siobhán trailed her fingertips up and down the outside of Annie's bare thigh, making her shiver.

"Did this happen with Laura?" Siobhán looked away, staring over Annie's body toward the window. "Siobhán?" Annie asked softly.

"It did." She sounded a little hoarse. "More or less, anyway. We fought about what her family would think if she came out. She made me think she was just waiting for the right time. And when we got to their house on the

97

Outer Banks, and I realized they had no idea we were a couple, and she had no intention of telling them otherwise, I lost my temper."

"What do you mean, you lost your temper?"

Siobhán wet her lips, and she still didn't meet Annie's gaze. "I did something I'm ashamed of."

"What was that?" Annie coaxed, apprehensive about what Siobhán's answer would be, but she needed to know.

"I—I made sure her parents knew—in vivid detail—what kind of relationship Laura and I had. I was cruel about it too."

"Oh, Siobhán," Annie reached out to pull her close. "You were hurting, and you lashed out. I'm not saying it was the right choice, but I'm sure you didn't mean to be cruel."

"It felt good," Siobhán said quietly. "Too good."

Annie stroked Siobhán's hair. "What happened after that?"

"Laura's father informed her that it was time for her dalliance to end." Siobhán shook her head. "That's what he called it. A two-year relationship with a woman I loved passionately. A woman I lived with. A woman I would have spent the rest of my life with if I could have." Siobhán's laugh was hollow. "A dalliance."

Annie's heart bled for Siobhán. "*That* was cruel," she said aloud.

"I suppose."

"What did Laura do?"

"Nothing," Siobhán's tone was flat. "She cried a lot. Told her father she loved me, but when he put his foot down and told Laura she had to pick between me and her family …"

"She picked her family," Annie said quietly.

"Yes." Siobhán looked away again. "Her family had money. I had none. I was still struggling then. It was before the Quinn Gallery started showing my work. When I met Laura, I was scraping by, living on tinned beans and toast in a tiny, run-down studio apartment, and wearing my coat inside so I could keep the heat as low as possible in the winter."

Annie winced. Boston winters were cruel. Annie had been living paycheck to paycheck lately, but it had never been that bad. And she knew if she got into a really serious jam, her parents would help. Her mother would never let her live it down, but she wouldn't let Annie starve.

Siobhán continued. "Laura's parents gave her a generous allowance. All she had to do was ask for more money, and they'd give it to her. So when we met, it just seemed natural for her to pay for things. She rented a nice apartment, and we moved in together. She lavished me with pretty clothes, and real furniture—not the broken futon and milk crates I'd been using before—and she bought us delicious meals and wine. I thought our life was perfect.

"I guess I shouldn't have expected her to pick me over her family, not when they could give her so much more. But after that fight, I went home to our apartment alone, and two days later, someone showed up to collect Laura's things. I think she felt guilty because the list she gave them barely included anything. She left most of it for me, even the furniture. I never saw her again or got to say a real goodbye. She was just ... gone. Back to her family, and that was the end of it. Of us."

"Oh, Siobhán. I'm so sorry."

Siobhán offered her a weak smile and flipped onto her back. "Every time I think I'm over her, something reminds me I'm not. When I heard you talking about how your mother felt, it hit a raw nerve. I love you, Annie, and I trust you, but sometimes I let my doubts get the better of me."

"We all do," Annie reassured her. "I have my doubts about myself that I'm working on."

Siobhán's smile didn't reach her eyes. "I hate to admit that woman has any control over me anymore."

"She hurt you badly," Annie said. "I understand."

"It really is ancient history. I don't know why I let it get to me like this."

Because you're still hurting over it, Annie thought. *And I don't know how to help.*

"I won't do that to you, you know," she said aloud. "My mother is being ridiculous, but no matter *what* she says, I'm not ending things, Siobhán. I care about you far too much to do that. I promise. You will always come first to me."

Siobhán offered her a tremulous smile. They lay there in silence for a few moments. All Annie could do was stroke her fingertips up and down Siobhán's arm and wonder if anything she could do would erase the hurt still inside Siobhán.

"This is nice," Siobhán said a while later, still staring up at the ceiling. "The light in here is beautiful."

Annie smiled as she flipped on her back to watch the sunlight through the trees make patterns on the wall and ceiling. "I've wanted to bring you here to see it for a while," she admitted. "It's the best part about living here."

"I can see why. It makes me feel at ease."

Siobhán reached out and took her hand. They lay there, fingers meshed together for a long time as the shadows lengthened and eventually the room grew dim. There were no sounds but the quiet rustle of the trees outside the half-open window and Siobhán's steady breathing.

"One good thing came about because of lunch with my parents, I guess," Annie said when she realized it was nearly dark. She sat up and clicked on the lamp beside the bed, blinking at the sudden wash of bright light.

"Coming here to your apartment?" Siobhán turned to look at her.

"That too. I meant that I'm even more determined to start the blog."

Siobhán sat up, looking much less sleepy all of a sudden. "That's wonderful."

"My mother was putting me down for not having my career figured out, and I blurted it out at her. It didn't impress her, but it made me realize I really want to do it," Annie admitted. "I'm *excited* about it."

Siobhán leaned in and kissed her. "Oh, Annie, that makes me so happy."

"You make me happy," Annie said softly.

A short while later, they ventured out into the apartment in search of food. Siobhán wore a T-shirt and pair of shorts that belonged to Annie, but she looked far better in them than Annie ever had.

100

"This is a cute little place," Siobhán murmured as they walked through the kitchen. "The hardwood floors are nice."

"It's not bad," Annie admitted, pleased to see that the room was spotless. To Annie's surprise, Trent had cleaned sporadically—if not terribly well—a few times recently. At the moment, the room looked immaculate, so she suspected Dee was home. And according to the sticky note that Annie saw on the fridge, there was a work order in for the super to come fix the dishwasher. It was huge progress.

"It would be a lot easier if I weren't living with three other people." She could hear the faint sound of voices coming from the direction of the living room. "I'm not sure who's home, but I'll introduce you to them."

As they approached the living room, Annie found Trent and Dee sitting on the couch. Dee was perched on Trent's lap, and they were laughing about something.

"Hey there, Annie," Dee said as they walked in. She moved as if to rise, but Trent wrapped his arms around her waist and—still laughing—she sat back down.

"Hey, long time no see, roomie," Annie said with a smile. "Dee, this is my girlfriend, Siobhán. Siobhán, this is Dee, the roommate who I rarely ever see. And that's her boyfriend Trent, who I see too much of."

Trent made a face. "Thanks."

"Lovely to meet you both," Siobhán said with a smile.

"Oooh, you got yourself an Irish girl," Dee said with a broad grin, her teeth flashing white against her deep brown skin. "Nicely done."

Annie laughed and took Siobhán's hand. She'd had no idea how Dee would react to her dating a woman, but it appeared Dee had no issues with it. "I'm pretty happy," she admitted.

"She's definitely hot," Trent said. "Not dyke-y at all."

Siobhán raised an eyebrow at him, but didn't say anything. Annie squeezed her hand. At least, Siobhán couldn't say Annie hadn't warned her about what an idiot Trent could be.

Dee craned her neck to look at her boyfriend. "That is the most asinine thing you've said all day, and that's saying something."

101

Annie snorted. "How do you stand him, Dee? I have yet to figure that out."

Dee grinned at her again. "Well, I think it's pretty similar to what I heard going on in your bedroom earlier. The man knows his way around a pussy. And I don't mean with his cock, although he's no slouch in that department either." Dee wasn't usually so blunt about sex, but maybe Trent's lack of filter had rubbed off on her.

"Damn it, Dee," Trent muttered. "I don't like to admit that."

Annie laughed loudly. So all of Trent's bluster about not eating pussy had just been stupid macho bullshit. She should have guessed.

"Now what is so wrong about admitting you're good at pleasing a woman?" Dee gave him a perplexed look.

"I'll admit I'm good at pleasing a woman," he said. "But people don't need to know *how*."

"You are so full of it." Dee rolled her eyes and turned back to face Annie and Siobhán. "What are you two up to today?"

"I introduced Siobhán to my parents. Not much else."

"How'd that go?"

Annie grimaced. "My mother was a jerk. My dad was pretty cool about things though."

"I can sympathize," Dee said. "My mom was okay with Trent, but my father damn near had a heart attack when I brought a white man home."

Annie feigned shock. "You mean you were brave enough to take him home to meet your parents? That's just crazy, Dee. He's barely fit for human interaction."

Dee snorted. "Isn't that the truth?"

"What is this? Gang up on Trent day?" he muttered.

"Oh that's every day, honey," Dee said. She finally extricated herself from Trent's grasp and he slapped her on the ass as she stood. "Besides, I know you like it."

Chapter Eleven

The next day, Annie and Siobhán spent a lazy morning in her bed, then ventured out again for food. They spotted Rebecca as they passed her open bedroom door.

"Hey there," she said, waving from where she was upside down doing some sort of exercise in the narrow space between her bed and the wall. Yoga? Pilates? Annie wasn't quite sure *what* she was doing, but it looked painful.

"Oh, hey, Rebecca. This is my girlfriend Siobhán. Siobhán, Rebecca."

She righted herself with a perky little hop. Annie wanted to swear at her for how impossibly perfect she looked even while working out. Annie was always red in the face and sweaty by the time she finished running. She tried not to wince when she thought about the last time she'd gone out for a run. Before she'd met Siobhán, actually. Whoops. She had a bad habit of letting it slide when she was in the new part of a relationship. Her mother had been on to something there, although Annie didn't think five pounds warranted the public criticism.

"Nice to meet you," Rebecca said. "What are you guys up to?"

"We're going out to grab breakfast." Annie glanced at the time on the clock on Rebecca's wall. "Um, or lunch."

Rebecca laughed. "Are you coming back here after?"

"I am," Annie explained. "Siobhán needs to go to her place to paint. She's an artist," Annie clarified, so Rebecca didn't think she was rolling paint on the walls.

"Oh, right. You guys met at a gallery, right?"

"Yes, we did," Siobhán said. "At one of my shows."

Rebecca beamed at them. "That's so romantic!"

Siobhán scoffed. "Maybe if I hadn't started off by swearing and insulting the gallery owner who I later found out is a friend of Annie's, it would have been."

Rebecca laughed. "Well, clearly, it worked anyway."

"What can I say? I'm a sucker for an Irish accent," Annie admitted. "Siobhán could have insulted my whole family, and I probably still would have been drooling, especially once I turned around and got a look at her."

"Aww, you guys are so sweet together!" Rebecca said.

Annie's stomach audibly rumbled with hunger. They'd snacked a little last night before bed but hadn't ever really had dinner. Apparently, her stomach was convinced she was starving. "And I think that's my cue it's time for me to eat," she said with a little laugh.

"Well, I won't keep you then," Rebecca said. "I'm going into work soon, but you guys have a nice day!"

"Thanks! You too," Annie offered her a genuine smile.

"I'm glad I got to come to your place," Siobhán said as they left the apartment. "It's nice to meet your roommates."

"Yeah, they're not so bad, I guess."

"Rebecca seems nice."

"She's growing on me," Annie admitted.

After Rebecca's dismissive behavior about her sexuality in the past, Annie hadn't been sure how Rebecca would treat Siobhán, but it was nice that she'd been friendlier lately. It seemed like Annie asking for help with her style had broken the ice between them a little.

"Actually, all of my roommates are kind of growing on me." Annie sighed when she realized she was the common denominator. "Or maybe I was just miserable before and projecting it onto them."

"Or maybe being in love means you're a little more tolerant of them," Siobhán said.

"Yeah, that's very possible."

It was a short walk to a nearby restaurant that served breakfast most of the day. They were quickly seated at a small table inside. Once they had coffee in front of them and their orders placed, Siobhán gave her a thoughtful look.

"Now that you're getting along with them better, would you miss your roommates if you moved in with me?"

"*When* I move in with you," Annie corrected. "And yeah, I'll probably miss them a little. Rebecca's been pretty great lately. I like Dee. And Trent can be kinda douchey, but he's growing on me. He's been a little better about washing his dishes lately, and we've come to a truce about the butter issue, which makes him a lot more tolerable."

"Butter issue? You mentioned that before but ..."

"Don't ask. Some weird diet thing of his."

Siobhán chuckled, but she grew serious after a moment. "Please don't take this the wrong way, Annie, but it seems like you don't have many close friends."

Annie sighed. "I guess I don't anymore. There are a few girls from college I stay in contact with. We grab dinner once a month or so. And a few people from the paper I see sometimes. I got into a bad habit of letting friendships slide when I was in a relationship. And then I felt too guilty after and never called people to apologize."

"I do that too," Siobhán said. "I get so wrapped up in the relationship, and I put all my energy into that and into my painting ... I don't think about anything else. People just drift away after a while."

"The other bad thing is that I haven't worked out since we met," Annie admitted. "I think I'll go for a run today maybe."

"Oh, you're a runner?" Siobhán made a face. "I try to do as little of that as possible."

Annie laughed, then groaned at the thought that Siobhán looked as gorgeous as she did with no effort. "Please don't tell me you're naturally that fit with no exercise."

Siobhán laughed. "I'm thirty-five, Annie. Believe me, I work at it. I just don't run. There's a gym around the corner from me with a pool. I swim laps and take aerobics classes when I remember to go."

"Well that's a relief," Annie joked. She sobered after a moment. "Do you think maybe we should both make an effort to get back to our normal lives though?"

Siobhán frowned. "Not if it means seeing less of you."

"Well, I don't want to cut into our time too much either, but we both admitted we're bad about maintaining our friendships and, well, our *health* when we get wrapped up in a relationship. Maybe it would be good if we both worked on that." Annie glanced down at the dark liquid in her coffee cup, not really seeing it. "I just don't want to do what I've always done before. I want this to be different."

I want this to last, she thought.

Siobhán reached out and took her hand. "I understand. I suppose I can let you out of my sight for a bit if it's in the name of your health and happiness." Her tone was light and teasing.

Annie gave her a look. "Oh, don't be so dramatic."

"I'm not trying to be!" Siobhán said with a laugh. "I just can't think of anything else but you when you're around, Annie."

"Believe me, I know the feeling," Annie said softly.

The conversation was cut short when a waitress dropped off Siobhán's eggs benedict and Annie's mushroom and tomato omelet, but it left a warm little glow inside Annie as they kissed goodbye and went their separate ways that afternoon.

After Annie returned from a long-overdue run, she showered and staggered to her bedroom to get some work done. Her phone rang a few minutes later. She picked it up, half-expecting it to be Siobhán, but it turned out to be her father.

"I'm sorry about your mother, Pumpkin," he said when she answered.

Annie sighed. "Thanks, Dad."

"Do you want me to have a talk with her and see if I can't get her to look at things a bit differently?"

"You're welcome to try. I'm not holding my breath though."

"You know your mother, Annie; she just wants what's best for you."

"Maybe. But Siobhán *is* what's best for me," Annie argued.

"I can see that. I can tell she cares about you."

"You approve then?"

"Why wouldn't I?" He sounded vaguely mystified.

"I just wanted to be sure."

"I like Siobhán. You seem happy, and I'm sorry your mother couldn't see that."

"Thanks, Dad." Annie was grateful to at least have one parent in her corner.

"Well, I'm gonna let you go. I just wanted you to know that I'm glad we got to meet your girlfriend. And I'll talk more to your mother. She'll come around in time, I'm sure."

"I hope so," Annie said with a sigh. "Thanks for calling."

"Sure thing. Talk to you soon, Pumpkin." He hung up without another word. He hated talking on the phone so Annie was surprised but pleased that he'd bothered to call at all.

Some of the anger at her mother had faded, replaced by a vague sense of irritation. She was just so *tired* of having to defend whatever relationship she was in. She'd told Siobhán she'd let friendships slide when she was in a relationship, but that wasn't really the whole story. A handful of the lesbian women she'd met through an LGBTQ center had dropped her the moment she'd gotten in a relationship with a man, and Annie hadn't bothered to go back to the center once she was single again. She'd never really felt like she'd belonged. It had been a bit easier when she was dating women, but even then, people had seemed a bit suspicious whenever Annie had identified as being bi. LGBTQ was supposed to represent bi people too, but somehow, it always seemed to get lost somewhere along the way.

Annie sighed and shook her head to clear it. Time to get to work. Lamenting the lack of community in her life wasn't going to help anything. And it certainly wasn't going to pay the bills.

That evening, she slid her key into Siobhán's lock and turned the knob. Siobhán looked up from the sofa as she stepped inside, and her quizzical face brightened when she spotted Annie. "I wondered who was breaking in!"

"Do you give your key to lots of women?" Annie asked with a smile. She'd considered knocking first, but that seemed odd and like it defeated the purpose of having a key of her own.

"No. I just didn't expect to see you tonight." Siobhán stood. She was wearing her favorite silk robe. It was Annie's favorite too.

"I decided to surprise you," Annie said. "I hope I'm not intruding."

"Of course not. I'm glad you're here." Siobhán leaned in to kiss her briefly, then took her bags. "I'll throw this in my room."

"Throw it carefully," Annie called after her as she kicked off her shoes. "My laptop's in there."

Siobhán returned a few moments later and patted the couch beside her. "Sit. Tell me about your day."

"It was pretty uneventful." Annie tucked her legs up under her. "I went for a run."

"Oh, good. I took your suggestion to heart and went to the pool after dinner. I just got out of the shower, in fact."

Siobhán's hair was still damp-looking, wetting the silk of her robe and leaving transparent spots in it.

"Good swim?" Annie asked.

"It served its purpose. How was your run?"

Annie grimaced. "It was rough. My mom was right that I've been slacking."

"You look wonderful to me," Siobhán said. "I thought her comment was ridiculous."

Annie squeezed her leg. "I appreciate that. I do need to keep at it though. When I'm actually running regularly, I enjoy it. It helps clear my head. Today was just rough because it had been a while. My muscles staged a protest."

"Remind me to give you a massage before we go to bed."

Annie nearly moaned aloud at the thought. "You don't have to tell me twice. That sounds like heaven. My calves are killing me."

"Did you get some work done today too?"

"Yes," Annie said. "In fact, I pulled together some more ideas for the blog."

"Wonderful!"

"How was your painting?"

"Oh, not bad. I made some good progress this afternoon. I should be done in a day or two."

"It seems like we both had a good day then." Annie smiled at her. "Oh, which reminds me, my Dad called to tell me he was sorry about the way lunch went. He said he'd talk to my mother and make her see reason."

"Do you think he'll be able to?"

Annie shrugged. "He seems to think so. I'm a little less convinced, but hopefully, he's right. My mother can be a pain, but she means well. Most of the time." Annie made a face.

"I know I wasn't there for what she said to you about us, but you don't want to give up on her completely," Siobhán said. "You won't always have the chance to fix it."

Annie frowned. "Siobhán, why don't you ever talk about your family?"

Siobhán let out a heavy sigh. "It's hard. Me ma is gone."

"Oh! It didn't have anything to do with The Troubles, did it?" Annie asked apprehensively. "You seemed ... subdued when you were talking about it at lunch with my parents."

"Oh, no. Her death had nothing to do with that. It was a hard time for a lot of families, but we were pretty well clear of it. I think an uncle of mine got mixed up in it at some point, but that was ancient history by the time I was born." Siobhán looked down at her hands. "No, me ma died while I was at university, actually."

"Oh, Siobhán." Annie's heart ached at the thought. "Were you close?"

109

BRIGHAM VAUGHN

"Very. She was the one who got me da to come around about me being a lesbian. He didn't like the idea at first. I'm not sure he ever was really happy with it, but he tolerated it for her."

"What happened?"

"To me ma?" Annie nodded. "Cancer. Breast cancer. She was always looking out for us, making sure everyone else was taken care of that she ignored the symptoms too long. By the time she got diagnosed, there wasn't much they could do for it. One minute she was there and then ..." Siobhán sighed. "And then she was gone."

Annie drew her closer. "I'm sorry. You must have been so young."

"I'd just turned twenty."

"I suppose any age is too young to lose your mother, but that's awful." As much as Annie wanted to strangle her mother at the moment, she couldn't stand the thought of losing her.

"Is the picture on the refrigerator of you and your parents?"

"Yes, just before I went off to university."

"Do you have any other pictures of her?" Annie asked.

"Yes. Would you like to see?"

"Please."

Siobhán crossed the room to the bookshelf and knelt down, returning to the couch a few moments later holding a small box. "I brought them with me when I moved. I didn't take much, but I had to take these with me."

"Of course. Come here and show me." Annie held out an arm, and Siobhán curled up against her.

Siobhán took a deep breath before she opened the box and pulled out a small stack of photos. She handed them to Annie one at a time. The first was of a young woman holding a tiny, bundled infant with dark hair. She looked exhausted but triumphant. "Is that the two of you?"

"No, actually." Siobhán craned her neck to look at Annie. "That was my mother with my older brother, Patrick. He died when he was a few months

110

old. Cot death. I think it's called something else now but that's what me ma called it when she talked about it."

"Sudden Infant Death Syndrome?" Annie guessed.

Siobhán nodded. "That's it."

"How horrible," Annie said softly. "I can't imagine. There was a kid I went to school with who lost his sister that way. The family never really seemed to recover."

"I don't know what my family was like before they lost Patrick, so I'll never really know how it changed them. I know my mother would get quiet sometimes for no reason. And she'd cry on his birthday, and we'd go to the cemetery to put flowers on the little headstone."

"How sad."

Siobhán handed her another picture. This one was clipped from a yellowed newspaper and was of a couple standing outside of what looked like a church. It was captioned *"Wedding of Sean Patrick Murray and Aileen Siobhán McCormack."*

"That's beautiful. You were named after her, then?"

Siobhán nodded and brushed her thumb over the aged paper. "I was."

The woman was young and beaming. The young man stared at her with a completely smitten expression.

"They look like they were in love," Annie commented.

"They were. He was crazy about her, and she did everything for him. They were in love right up until her last breath."

Annie smiled sadly. "She's beautiful. You look just like her."

"Thank you. And yes, I know I do. That's why he couldn't stand to have me around after she was gone." Siobhán's voice sounded raw. "He said lookin' at me was like starin' at a ghost."

"Oh, Siobhán. How awful. How could he do that when you were both hurting?"

"I don't really blame him. He might not have died but he became something like a ghost himself," Siobhán said grimly.

"Did he drink?" Annie asked.

Siobhán's eyes flashed as she shot Annie a hard look. "Why? You assume he's a drunk because he's Irish?"

"No. Of course not." Annie soothed her with a gentle touch on her leg. "It's just common that when someone loses someone, they turn to something to numb the pain. Alcohol's a pretty common choice. Pretty much anywhere in the world."

"Sorry. I can be a bit tetchy about that." Siobhán sighed. "No, he didn't drown his sorrows in a pint down at the pub like a lot of men. He hardly ever drank before, and me ma's death didn't change that. He just got surlier and surlier. I'd go to visit, and he'd barely look up from the television screen as he watched rugby and football. He'd just grunt his answers and ignore me."

"That must have hurt."

Siobhán nodded. "I needed him and he just … wasn't there."

Annie reached out and squeezed her leg, this time leaving her hand in place. "What did you do?"

"Ran away to Boston," Siobhán said flatly. "Packed my bags, booked a flight, and left without saying goodbye."

"Have you talked since?"

"A few times a year. My birthday. Christmas. Sometimes I wonder if he only does it because he's afraid me ma is lookin' down at him from heaven and scolding 'im."

"Do you miss him?"

"Every day."

"Have you been home since?"

"To Bray?"

"Yes."

"No." Siobhán looked away. "I flew to Dublin to see my childhood friend get married. I asked my father to meet me there. He never came. I didn't go home again after that."

"I'm so sorry, Siobhán."

"I lost me ma and me da all in the same year," Siobhán said softly. "And it never stops hurting."

Annie drew her close, her heart aching for all that Siobhán and her family had been through.

Chapter Twelve

September

Annie slipped the simple diamond studs her parents had bought her for her college graduation into her ears and stepped back to give herself a critical look.

"Are you sure this looks okay?" she asked, smoothing the black dress over her hips. It was sleeveless, hit below her knees and had an interesting asymmetric neckline. The dress had been purchased at a second-hand store. Rebecca had been in raptures about the designer—although Annie had never heard of them before—and assured her the dress was stylish and no would ever know where she got it.

"You look great," Rebecca said. "I promise."

"My hair certainly looks amazing," Annie admitted. "You really are a genius at it."

Rebecca had swept her hair up into a loose bun at the back of her neck and made it look like Annie had much fuller, thicker hair that she really did. She'd also done Annie's make up and her eyes looked huge and vibrantly blue. Her cheeks had a faint flush, and her lips were a glossy rose color.

She felt better about her look for the evening than she had when she'd begged Rebecca for help a few weeks ago, but she was still nervous about her date with Siobhán that evening. They were going to a private event at the Quinn Gallery.

It was closed to the public that night, but Gabriel was throwing one of his semi-annual dinner parties. Annie had heard about them—though never been invited—and Gabriel had practically insisted that Siobhán come. Annie was her guest.

She hated making conversation at parties like this—especially since her career was so unsure at the moment. It was one thing to say she was a journalist, but a freelance writer always sounded so vague and pathetic. An aspiring blogger wasn't any more impressive.

At least, the blog was starting to come together. Annie had picked out a theme and built the basic pages. She'd even written up a number of posts. Siobhán was nearly finished with the painting for the banner and once that was done and Annie was sure everything was in place, she'd hit publish.

The thought gave her butterflies in her stomach. All she could do was hope it wouldn't be a complete flop.

A knock on the door startled her. "That's probably Siobhán," she said. "Thanks, Rebecca, I owe you."

"It was fun!" Rebecca said with a smile.

"Good because I may need your help again in the future," Annie admitted. She heard another knock on the door. "Gotta run though."

Annie scooped up the robin's egg blue silk shawl and beaded clutch Rebecca had loaned her on her way out of the room. She was a little breathless when she answered the door. "Sorry, Siobhán. Come on in for a sec while I put on my shoes."

Siobhán stared at her open-mouthed. "Jaysus, Annie. You look …"

Annie flushed with pleasure. "You like? Rebecca helped."

"You're stunning. I'm not going to be able to keep my hands off you tonight." Siobhán stepped inside and closed the door after her.

"Well, you better," Annie teased. "I think I mentioned that public exhibition isn't my thing."

Siobhán sighed heavily. "If you insist. But I can't promise I won't drag you into Gabriel's office and have my way with you at some point. The door will be locked, but that's the best I can manage."

Annie shivered at the thought. "You're a little bit evil, you know that?"

Siobhán gave her a triumphant smile. "So the nuns used to tell me."

Annie chuckled. "I'll be thinking about that all evening you know."

"Good."

115

Annie took a long look at Siobhán.

She had on a long, black gauzy dress. It had spaghetti straps and slits up to mid-thigh on either side. It was somehow hip and elegant at once, and with red heels, a sculptural silver necklace, and minimal makeup except for a slash of red lipstick, she looked completely stunning. And completely out of Annie's league.

"You look incredible too. God, you could be bringing anyone tonight."

Siobhán looped her arm through Annie's. "And I'm bringing *you*."

"I can't imagine why," Annie said faintly. How on earth she'd attracted a woman like Siobhán Murray was beyond her. But she was glad she had.

"Because I love you, *ya bleedin' eejit*." Siobhán frowned. "Damn it, I shouldn't have worn red lipstick. I really want to kiss you, but I'll make a mess of us both if I do."

Siobhán's phone buzzed and she started. "And I've nearly forgotten about the Lyft car I have waiting. Are you ready, Annie?"

"Let me grab my shoes." Annie dashed to her room and grabbed the staggeringly tall heels off her bed where she'd left them earlier.

She returned to the entryway where Siobhán was texting something on her phone. "I've let the driver know we're on our way down."

Annie took a seat on the little bench and slipped her shoes on. "How do they look?" she said when she stood. She rarely wore them, but they looked great with the dress.

Siobhán let out a low moan. "They look like you need to wear them with your legs draped over my shoulders," she said with a gleam in her eye.

"I thought it was just men who were obsessed with high heels," Annie said with a laugh. She draped the scarf around her shoulders, grabbed her purse, and opened the apartment door.

Siobhán followed. "I couldn't care less what men think of them. I think they make those legs of yours look about a mile long. I'll have to beat people off of you all night."

Annie chuckled. Unlikely, but she appreciated the compliment.

116

They were silent as they negotiated the two floors of stairs in heels and dresses, and Annie was reminded why she rarely wore them. Her feet were going to kill her by the end of the night, but Siobhán's reaction had been worth it.

"You seem a little tense," Siobhán said a short while later as they were in the Lyft car, speeding toward the Quinn Gallery.

"I am," Annie admitted. "I know the night's important for you, and you said you were going to talk to Gabriel about shooting the painting for my blog and …" She sighed. "It's just a little nerve-racking. Normally, I go to gallery shows, enjoy the art, and go home. This is a dinner party, and I'll have to spend all evening convincing people I'm less boring than I actually am."

Siobhán scoffed. "You worry too much. You can carry on a very intelligent conversation about art, you look stunning, and most of the people there will be half-drunk by the time they clear the salad plates. I'm thrilled that you're the one on my arm tonight."

Annie reached out and squeezed her hand. "You always manage to make me feel better," she admitted.

"Good," Siobhán said. "Now, I want you to relax and enjoy yourself tonight."

An hour later, Annie had to admit Siobhán had been right. The cocktail hour was going smoothly, and Annie had been enjoying talking with most of the people there. Siobhán had helped ease her into conversation with a few people she knew, and Annie found herself enthusiastically discussing her blog plans as she sipped champagne and nibbled at the artfully prepared canapes.

"No, no, I think it's great," David—a sculptor Annie had been chatting with for a short while—said. "I can't think of anything else that's exactly like what you're doing."

"Well, good," Annie said with a laugh. "I hope you'll tell everyone you know about it."

"Oh, definitely," he said.

She was aiming for a mix of out-of-town readers planning trips to Boston and locals looking to spend some time exploring their own city. She had a feeling the latter group would be the hardest to draw in, so she was hoping word-of-mouth would help.

The clinking of silverware on a glass caught Annie's attention. Gabriel stood nearby, and when the crowd quieted, he spoke. "Thank you all for coming this evening. I'm delighted you could all be here."

He had exchanged his usual fedora for a top hat tonight, along with a collared shirt—open at the neck—trousers, and a fancy waistcoat. The look seemed silly and over-the-top to her, but Gabriel had always had a flair for the dramatic.

It was a shame he could be so pompous because he really was rather good-looking. His thick brown hair and artful stubble contrasted nicely against the pallor of his skin, and his eyes were dark and soulful. In college, Annie had found him quite attractive.

"These parties are designed to be a fest for the eyes and a feast for the senses. So, please, take a seat, enjoy your meal, and then browse—and buy— the art you see here."

The crowd laughed and slowly dispersed. She half-listened as she surveyed the other guests taking their seats. She had to hand it to Gabriel; he *was* good at what he did. Siobhán raved about how well her paintings sold through his gallery, and Annie knew his name carried some serious weight in the local art community.

"Do you want to find our seats?" Siobhán murmured.

Annie turned to her with a smile. "Yes. Let's."

As they approached the long table dotted with bright, modern flower arrangements in low vases that stretched through the gallery, Annie admired the length of white linen, the gleam of silverware, and the sparkle of glassware. It really was gorgeous.

They peered at the escort cards—clever little easel-shaped pieces of cardboard with names written on them in fancy script—until they located their places. To her surprise, Annie realized she and Siobhán had been seated near the head of the table.

"Thank you for inviting me," Annie murmured to Gabriel after she sat.

"Of course." He beamed at her. "You're one of my oldest friends, Siobhán is one of my most successful artists, and the two of you make such a darling couple. Really, you'll have to toast me at your wedding and thank me for introducing you two."

Annie chuckled. "You hardly introduced us, Gabriel. Siobhán was the one who approached *me*."

"Still, my show set the stage," he boasted.

"Pretentious twat," Siobhán mouthed from across the table, her lips hidden from Gabriel behind the curtain of her hair.

Annie smothered a laugh at the reminder of Siobhán's opening line and reached for her wine glass. "Well, we certainly owe you for that." Since their relationship had begun with Siobhán poking fun at Gabriel, maybe they did owe him a big thank you. Probably best if they didn't tell him the specifics though.

Siobhán grinned at Annie from across the table and pushed her hair behind her shoulder. "Speaking of favors, I have one for you, Gabriel."

He raised an eyebrow at her. "Anything for you. What is it? Are you hoping for an extension on your next show because you've been too busy with this lovely creature to paint?"

Siobhán laughed. "Not at all. My paintings are coming along nicely. I'll have everything ready in time. No, this is personal."

"Sure, sure. What is it?"

"Well, Annie and I are collaborating on a project," Siobhán said.

Gabriel looked puzzled as he scrutinized her. "I didn't know you were a painter, Annie."

She laughed. "I'm not. Siobhán is the only one doing the painting."

Gabriel snapped his fingers. "Oh, does this have something to do with the blog I heard you talking about with someone earlier?"

"Yes," Annie said, relieved that she had a starting point. "I'm starting a blog about Boston travel and sightseeing. Siobhán is painting the Boston skyline for me to use as a banner. We wanted to ask you about using your equipment to photograph the piece so we can have a high-resolution copy for the page."

"I love that! Of course, you can use it." Gabriel leaned forward. "My only question is if there's any way I'll be able to get my hands on the painting."

Siobhán laughed. "That was *my* next question. My thought was that we'd feature the painting here in the gallery for a while. Not sell it—at least for six months or so—and draw people into your gallery to see it. Here at the gallery, you can direct people to Annie's blog. And then make a huge deal out of the sale of the painting once we do sell it."

"A"—Gabriel motioned with his hand as if searching for the word—"cross promotion of sorts."

"Exactly!" Annie grinned at him. "Is that something you'd be interested in? The blog will be small at first, but I'm confident I'll be able to get readership up. I can feature the Quinn Gallery in a post—with a disclaimer of course, so everything's above board—and draw more people in that way. It might take a little while, but I think it'll be beneficial for both of us."

Gabriel waved off her concerns. "Of course, of course. I remember your work in college. You certainly have the writing chops for it. The official city tourism sites never quite hit the mark. It's great that there's a listing of what's available, but what people could really use is in-depth reviews and a mobile guide. It's brilliant, really."

"Thank you, Gabriel," Annie said, feeling grateful. She laid a hand on his arm. "You have no idea how much I appreciate your support. With your gallery on board, I should be able to attract some other notable advertising."

Gabriel seemed to puff up at her praise. "Well, I like to lend my name where it can do some good."

Annie was tempted to roll her eyes at how pompous he was being, but she refrained. She was too damn grateful. She shot a glance at Siobhán, who she knew must be feeling the same way. But Siobhán's lips were tight as she stared at Annie's hand on Gabriel's arm.

Annie stifled a sigh and fought the instinct to pull away. She didn't want to act like she'd done anything wrong. Did Siobhán really think Annie had been flirting with Gabriel? She'd just been excited about the possible collaboration. It was ridiculous that Siobhán got so jealous sometimes. She'd been so much better lately, too.

Annie turned back to Gabriel with a smile. "Well, I appreciate your help. I think this will be a fantastic collaboration for all of us." She let go of him and sat back.

"Oh, definitely." He glanced over at Siobhán and lifted a glass to her and winked. "To collaboration with two gorgeous women! Something I'd like to do a lot more of."

Several people around them chuckled. Siobhán clinked her glass on his, her expression suddenly wooden. Her gaze seemed to pass right over Annie as they toasted. *Shit*, Annie thought, wondering how the wonderful evening had taken such a quick turn. *This isn't going to end well.*

"It wouldn't be the first time Annie and I collaborated on something, huh?" This time Gabriel winked and nudged her elbow.

Annie laughed uncomfortably. "I guess you could say that. But it was a million years ago, Gabriel, let's not bore everyone."

"I don't know," Siobhán said archly. "I'm not bored."

Don't do this, Siobhán, Annie pleaded with her eyes as she stared at her girlfriend. *Please, don't do this now.*

"Well, I've known Annie since college, you know," Gabriel boasted.

Annie cringed.

"I dated her roommate ... what was her name, Annie?"

"Sylvia," Annie said quietly.

"Yeah, yeah, Sylvia. She was a hot little piece. She and Annie both were. And I should know." Gabriel winked. "The three of us had some crazy times together."

He had a fond look on his face as he gazed off into space.

"Just the one time." Annie cleared her throat. "And, seriously, no one wants to hear about that."

Gabriel scoffed. "Come on, Annie. You used to be fun!"

121

"Yeah, well, I also used to be twenty-one, but both were a long time ago. My crazy days ended when I stopped doing bar crawls and tequila shots," she said drily.

He laughed. "Hey, I'm sure we can scrounge up some tequila tonight! You sure you're not just a little bit bi, Siobhán? Annie sure convinced Sylvia to play on both teams. Damn, that was fun."

Annie gritted her teeth together and glanced over to see a stony-faced Siobhán staring at Gabriel as if she could bore holes through his head with her glare.

Fuck, Annie thought. *How do I fix this?*

"I promise you, I'm not the faintest bit interested in that, Gabriel," Siobhán said. She stood, nearly toppling over her chair. "In fact, I'm not feeling very well. You'll have to excuse me."

She grabbed her phone and strode toward the door, the chiffon of her dress billowing dramatically around her legs. She pushed open the front door and disappeared onto the street.

The sudden murmuring of the people around them made Annie realize that everyone had been watching their little exchange.

Humiliated, tears rose to her eyes, and she stood on wobbly knees. "I'm going to go check on Siobhán, Gabriel. You'll have to excuse us."

"Shit, did I say something wrong?" He looked suddenly remorseful. "I didn't mean to."

"It's a little late for apologies," Annie said tersely. "The damage is already done."

She scooped up her shawl from the back of her chair, grabbed her purse, and then spotted Siobhán's purse on the table beside her abandoned plate. Well, at least, without that Siobhán wouldn't make it far.

When Annie left the gallery, she found Siobhán pacing on the sidewalk in front of the building.

"What exactly did Gabriel mean by that?" Siobhán snapped. She took her purse from Annie's outstretched hand.

122

Annie swallowed. "Exactly what it sounded like."

"You're going to have to be a little clearer than that."

She sighed heavily. "It was just harmless college experimentation. Gabriel was dating my roommate Sylvia for a while. One night, the three of us had a little too much to drink, and he coaxed Sylvia into kissing me. One thing led to another and ..." Annie laughed uncomfortably. "We hooked up. It was kinda fun at the time, but things were a bit awkward for a while after. I don't even know why he brought it up tonight."

"Well, he did. And now I'm left wondering when you were going to spring it on me that you aren't satisfied with our relationship!"

Staggered by Siobhán's statement, all Annie could do was blink at her for a moment. "Oh, don't be ridiculous, Siobhán! When have I ever acted like I was unsatisfied?"

"I don't know, maybe around the same time you weren't telling me you'd slept with Gabriel!"

"I didn't think it mattered!"

"I don't like knowing Gabriel Quinn has probably been sniggering behind my back about the fact that he fucked my girlfriend before I did."

"You're making something out of nothing," Annie said with a sigh. "Really Siobhán. I don't think he's been snickering about *anything*. It was some tasteless reminiscing, that's all."

"We're in complete agreement about how tasteless it was, at least," Siobhán muttered. "And I don't appreciate having that news sprung on me in the midst of a dinner party!"

A stab of guilt went through her. "You knew about the ones I had with Brigid and Nora."

"Those were different, Annie!"

"Why? Because they were with two women?"

"No, because they weren't with the man who sells my work," Siobhán hissed. "You should have told me!"

123

"Yeah, maybe I should have," Annie admitted. "Except there were a lot of reasons why it didn't seem like a good idea."

"Like what?" Siobhán crossed her arms over her chest.

"Like the fact that it's *Gabriel*, and I'm kinda embarrassed to admit I hooked up with him. Not to mention the fact that he *is* someone you work with and someone we have to deal with in the future. And … and because I know how you feel about bisexual women. And it didn't leave me with the feeling that you'd be very open-minded about things." Annie sighed heavily.

"Well, if I felt like I could trust bisexual women, it would be different!"

"Is this about Laura?" Annie snapped. Siobhán looked away, unable to meet her eye. "Jesus. Of course, it is!" Annie threw up her hands. "*Everything* seems to be about her."

"I'm not the one who had a bleeding threesome with my college roommate and her boyfriend!" Siobhán shouted.

"Well, I'm not going to apologize for one night that meant nothing and took place almost fifteen years ago," Annie shouted back. "This is *ridiculous*, Siobhán, and I'm tired of your jealousy. And I'm tired of living with the ghost of Laura hanging over us."

A car slid to a stop in front of them, and Annie groaned when Siobhán's phone vibrated in her hand. "Looks like your ride is here," she snapped.

"*My* ride?"

Annie sighed and fished through her purse for her phone. "I'll have another car pick me up and take me home."

"To your place?"

"Yes. I really don't feel like going home with you right now."

Siobhán looked at her with a hurt expression. "Fine. But don't be absurd. The driver can drop you off at your place, then take me to mine."

Annie hesitated, but it did seem pointless and stupid to wait for another ride. "Fine," she said with a sigh.

Once Siobhán told the driver the instructions, they rode to Annie's place in silence. Annie got out of the car but leaned in to look at Siobhán before she

124

closed it behind her. "I'm sorry things were such a mess tonight. Let's sleep on things and I'll ... I'll call you tomorrow, okay?"

Siobhán nodded but didn't say anything else. Annie closed the door behind her and stepped back.

As the car pulled away, she stared at Siobhán's face, faintly illuminated through the dark window. Annie was left alone, her heart aching.

Chapter Thirteen

"I owe you an apology."

Annie stared at her mother across the table, exhausted from the lack of sleep after her fight with Siobhán. She didn't know why she'd agreed to meet her mother for lunch when she'd called that morning. Her patience was already thin. "Do you *actually* feel sorry, or did Dad convince you to come here and apologize?"

Heather flushed and looked away. "Both, if you must know."

"Mom ..."

"No. You were right the other day. I shouldn't have said what I did. I was just taken aback. You've never been serious about a woman like this before." She sounded defensive.

"I've had a number of girlfriends over the years," Annie said, confused. She ripped off a small piece of bread and ate it. She hadn't been able to stomach breakfast, but she needed something in her or the wine she'd ordered would go right to her head.

"I assumed they were just an occasional fling. I certainly never thought you'd *settle down* with one. You didn't introduce us to them before."

"I'm sure you met a few of my girlfriends in college," Annie said with a puzzled frown, trying to recollect some specific instances. "Don't you remember Alicia?"

"Was that the brunette who helped us move you into the dorms at Northwestern? She lived down the hall from you or something."

"Two floors below me, but yes."

"Annie, I never realized she was your *girlfriend.* I simply thought she was a female friend who was very helpful."

"Oh." Annie felt vaguely idiotic for assuming her mother had picked up on that. "Well, she definitely was my girlfriend. We dated for four months."

"I don't think you ever specifically introduced us to a woman you were … involved with. I have distinct memories of you introducing us to Mark as your boyfriend years ago. And a few months later, you two moved in together."

"What does that have to do with my relationship with Siobhán?"

"Seeing you and Siobhán together … well, it made me realized you were serious about her."

"And you have a problem with that?" Annie tried to keep her tone neutral. She took another sip of wine.

"Well, I don't love it," Heather admitted. "It's just not the life I saw for you."

The words hurt and made her furious at the same time, but Annie forced herself to take a few slow, deep breaths before she responded. "But I'm happy."

"You couldn't be as happy with a man?"

"I couldn't be as happy without Siobhán," she explained. Despite the fight last night, her love for Siobhán hadn't dimmed. Annie *missed* her. She knew they had a lot to work on, but she was no more done with Siobhán than she was done breathing. "Look, being happy has nothing to do with the gender of the person I'm with, Mom. It's about being in love with someone who loves me back. Who wants to make me happy. Who brings out the best in me. I want what you and Dad have."

Heather folded her hands together, her diamond wedding ring sparkling in the sunlight. "And Siobhán makes you happy?"

"Yes," Annie said. "There are a few things we need to work on, but she truly does. I know you scoffed at my idea of starting a website—it's a blog really—but Siobhán's the one who encouraged me to find something I love to do. Something I'm passionate about."

"And that couldn't be journalism?" Heather said with a sigh. "We invested so much in your career, Annie. We just want you to live up to your potential."

127

"I know that, Mom." Annie tried to keep her voice gentle. "But look at it this way. If I start this blog, it will be similar to journalism. I'll be using the skills I was taught in school. I'll be doing research, writing articles, trying to hook readers … it's not so far off. There are already people excited about advertising on it."

Well, that might be stretching things, actually. She had no idea if the argument with Siobhán had soured Gabriel's interest in working with her. She'd have to straighten that out soon, although Gabriel was the last person she felt like talking to at the moment.

Heather's expression was dubious. "And you'd really enjoy this … this *blogging?*"

"I really think I would," she admitted.

"And it could generate income? I don't want you racking up credit card debt for some pipe dream."

"I'm doing everything I can to make sure it pays the bills. I don't know. Maybe it won't be a success. But I want to *try*. And for the first time, I'm really excited about my future. About the blog, about being with Siobhán … it's been a long time since I've feel this happy, Mom."

She sighed. "Well, then, I wish you luck. I do want you to be happy, Annie. I hope you know that."

"Thanks, Mom." Annie reached out and squeezed her mom's fingers. "That means a lot to me."

Heather took a sip of her drink. "And tell Siobhán we'd like to have you both over for dinner. If she's going to be around, we'll have to get to know her better."

"I'd like that," Annie said. "I'd really, really like that, Mom."

"And—and I'll apologize to her for my poor behavior," she added.

Annie reached out and grabbed her mom's hand. "Thank you. That means the world to me."

Heather sighed. "You know, you expect a lot of people, Annie."

"Yeah, I suppose I do," she admitted.

Annie's phone rang shortly after she left the restaurant. She was disappointed to realize it wasn't Siobhán, and the sight of Gabriel's name popping up on her screen didn't really improve her mood.

She took a deep breath and accepted the call anyway. She might as well rip the bandage off and get it over with. "Hello."

"Oh, Annie. I'm so glad I caught you."

"Look, Gabriel, I want to apologize about last night," she said. "I'm sorry Siobhán and I disappeared like that and—"

"No, no!" He protested. "I'm calling because *I* need to apologize. I was kinda drunk, and I totally stuck my foot in my mouth. I never thought about the fact that Siobhán might not already know about what happened and ... I figured it would be something we'd all laugh about. Shit, I feel so guilty."

"It's okay, Gabriel. Obviously, it was a bigger issue for Siobhán than I realized. I don't think any of us really reacted well," Annie said with a sigh. "I appreciate the apology though."

"Yeah, of course. I like you guys. I hope it didn't cause too big of a problem."

"We'll work it out," Annie assured him, hoping that was true. She couldn't imagine what would happen if they didn't work through it. Life without Siobhán seemed so bleak.

"Good. Glad to hear it." Gabriel was silent for a moment. "Are we still on for doing the cross-promotion then?"

Annie paused as she wondered if *that* was why Gabriel had really called. No doubt, felt guilty about sparking a fight between her and Siobhán, but in the end, he was probably more worried about his business than their friendship—such as it was. Then again, Annie supposed she wasn't any different. She'd been more worried about the possible impact on her blog than any relationship she had with him.

"Yeah, we should be," she said. "I'll talk to Siobhán about the painting, but I don't see why we can't keep moving forward with that."

"Fantastic!" Gabriel sounded relieved. "That'll be great for both of us. All of us, really."

"Yeah, I think so," Annie agreed.

"I actually talked to a couple friends to see if they were interested. I figured if you were too mad, I could tell you it was a peace offering."

"Oh?" Annie asked, surprised. Maybe he really *did* feel bad about the way things had gone the night before. Or maybe he just didn't want to piss off the girlfriend of one of his most successful artists. Siobhán was established enough to take her work anywhere. Gabriel wouldn't want to risk losing that. It certainly worked in Annie's favor.

"Yeah, I'll email all of the info to you, but there's a wine bar and restaurant interested in advertising too. And I may have an in with someone at a museum, but I'll have to get back to you on that."

"Thank you," Annie said sincerely. Whatever Gabriel's motivation, she really appreciated the effort he'd put in. "I really appreciate you doing this. And your confidence that this blog will be worth supporting is really nice."

Gabriel scoffed. "I meant what I said last night about your writing, Annie. I remember the pieces in *The Boston Chronicle* you did, and they were damn good," he said, referring to the newspaper she'd written for. "You're a talented writer. I'm really looking forward to the blog."

"Thanks, Gabriel. That means a lot."

"So everything's okay?"

"Yeah, everything's fine," Annie said with a faint smile as she said goodbye and hung up the phone.

Maybe he *was* a bit of a pompous boor about art sometimes. And his fashion choices left something to be desired. But Annie was starting to think he was a better friend than she'd realized—loose tongue aside—and she wondered if she'd been a little unfair to him.

She sighed when she realized that was the theme for the day. Maybe she needed to re-evaluate the way she treated the people in her life.

The question now was: had she expected too much of Siobhán?

She'd planned to call Siobhán when she got home, but instead, she sent a quick text asking if she could come over. They needed to clear the air and see if they could find a way to work through the fight. There was less chance of a miscommunication if they spoke in person.

She got a one-word response, but it gave her hope. *Please.*

Half an hour later, Annie knocked on Siobhán's door, her heart in her throat. She'd spent the time on the subway and walk from the station trying to figure out what she was going to say, but the moment Siobhán answered the door, all of the words fled.

"Hey," Siobhán said. She seemed unusually subdued, and the corners of her mouth trembled when she tried to smile. It made Annie's heart ache.

"Hey," Annie said softly. "Can I come in?"

"Of course." Siobhán opened the door wider and stepped back.

They stood there staring at each other for a moment after the door had closed. Before Annie could formulate another word, Siobhán threw her arms around Annie.

"I'm sorry," she said, her voice muffled by Annie's shoulder. "I'm so fecking sorry, Annie."

Annie hugged Siobhán against her. "Me too."

Siobhán pulled back and wiped at her damp eyes. "What do you have to be sorry about?"

"I should have talked to you about what happened with Gabriel. A part of me knew you'd be upset by it, and I was avoiding that." She tugged Siobhán over toward the couch.

"Well, if I wouldn't fly off the handle every time something comes up, maybe you wouldn't feel that way," Siobhán muttered.

"It would help," Annie admitted. "I get it, Siobhán; you're a passionate person. And we *both* have a bit of a temper. But I don't want to fight all the time."

"No, I don't either." Siobhán frowned. "Can you forgive me, Annie?"

"Of course. But I do think we need to talk about something."

Siobhán sighed heavily. "Laura?"

"Yeah."

131

"I know." Siobhán rubbed her wrist. "I don't mean for her to be hanging over us, Annie; I swear."

"I know you don't. It's just ... it seems like there are three of us in this relationship right now, and I never wanted that."

"Me either." Siobhán let out a frustrated sigh. "I just don't know how to get rid of her, Annie. I never got to say goodbye. I never got any closure. I swore to myself I'd never date another bi woman and ..."

"And I'm a bisexual woman." Annie made a face. "I just wish I could understand why it makes such a difference, Siobhán."

Siobhán's eyes looked huge and sad as she stared at Annie. "Because a part of me is always afraid you'll decide I'm not enough."

Annie stared at her in shock. "Siobhán, that's never going to be an issue."

"You say that now, but how do I know you aren't going to decide that you need something I can't give you?"

"Like *what?*" Annie asked. "A dick?"

"Well, yeah."

"Oh, for fuck's sake, Siobhán!" Annie said. "How can you possibly think that matters?"

"I don't know, Annie. There's obviously something you like about men!"

"Well, I don't mind a good dick," Annie admitted. "But only if it's attached to someone I care about! *That's* the part that matters. Why is that so hard for people to grasp? I had the same discussion with my mother today."

Siobhán blinked at her. "You talked to your mother?"

"Yes," Annie said. "And we smoothed things over. She wants to have us over for dinner and to apologize to you."

"You were still planning things for our future even though I've been horrible to you?"

"You have to be kidding me." Annie stared up at the ceiling for a moment. "Of course, I was! I never thought this was the end of things. I was just mad and frustrated. But don't change the subject."

"Sorry."

"Listen to me about this, Siobhán. I don't care what your gender is. What's between your legs or anywhere else. I want *you*. You stubborn, hot-headed Irish woman." Annie blinked back tears. "I love you."

Tears spilled down Siobhán's cheeks. "I love you too. And I'm trying to understand."

"I know you are."

"I just went crazy when I heard Gabriel talking about you and your roommate, and I started to doubt everything. What if six months from now you decide you need a threesome?"

Annie stared at her in shock for a moment. The idea was absurd to her. She had enjoyed the ones in college, but they had just been flings. Never with anyone she was in love with. That was a world away from what she had with Siobhán. She couldn't imagine sharing Siobhán with anyone else, but she knew it was something Siobhán was genuinely worried about, and she hastened to reassure her.

"Trust me; it isn't some huge kink of mine. It was silly experimenting in college. Yes, I enjoyed the ones with Brigid and Nora, but it never meant anything. And the one with—with Gabriel was fun until the next morning when we sobered up, and then it just made everything awkward. I haven't had one since as none of them meant anything. It isn't something I want, Siobhán, much less *need*."

"Oh."

Annie gave her a quizzical look. "Did you really think I was running around having a bunch of threesomes before I met you?"

"No, not really," Siobhán said with a sigh. "I just couldn't stop the little voice wondering if you'd feel like you were missing out on it in the future."

"I won't. I promise," she said firmly.

"I could use a strap-on sometime if you wanted," Siobhán offered.

Annie chuckled. "You can if you want sometime. I'm not opposed to the idea. But it's not because I want it to be a dick. I don't care how you fuck me. All I need, all I want, is *you*, Siobhán."

133

"I believe you." Siobhán reached out and drew Annie toward her. She came willingly until she was stretched out on top of Siobhán. "I love you so fecking much, Annie."

"I love you too." Annie kissed her with all of the fervent, pent-up passion from their argument. When Siobhán shifted so she lay between Annie's legs, worshiping Annie's mouth with her own, Annie felt the tension that had been in her since the night before finally fade.

But in a small, distant corner of her mind, she wondered if they'd put Laura's ghost to rest or if she was still lurking there.

Waiting to disrupt their happiness again.

Chapter Fourteen

"**M**orning, *mo álainn*," Siobhán whispered in her ear. They were lying on their sides, spooned together.

"Morning," Annie said sleepily.

Siobhán slid a hand over Annie's hip and gently coaxed Annie's legs apart. She moaned when Siobhán's fingers met the slightly aching flesh between her legs. She and Siobhán had spent half the night making love. She should have felt thoroughly content and uninterested in anything more, but the feel of Siobhán gently stimulating her made her moan.

"Does that feel good, Annie?" Siobhán said, her lips feathering against Annie's neck and making her shiver.

The best Annie could manage was another low moan of pleasure. She hooked her leg on top of Siobhán's, who took full advantage of the increased access to Annie's body. Siobhán delved deeper, gently sliding two fingers into her. She was wet—either from the night before or from what Siobhán had just been doing—and she accepted the intrusion of her fingers easily.

Annie whimpered when Siobhán bit at her shoulder, and she contracted around Siobhán, moving her hips to encourage Siobhán to go deeper. The sweet, slow strokes pushed her higher and higher, and her whole body tensed in anticipation.

"Are you close, *mo grá*?"

"Yes," Annie managed to gasp. Siobhán pressed closer and slid her free arm under Annie's body so she could tease Annie's nipples. When she cupped Annie's pubic mound and fucked Annie with her fingers, it sent Annie quickly spiraling over the edge. She cried out loudly, her entire body shaking with the force of her orgasm.

Everything went white and fuzzy, and for a few moments, she lay there gasping. Her head was buried in the pillow, and Siobhán was wrapped tightly around her.

"Jesus, Siobhán," she managed when she lifted her head. "The things you do to me …"

"You love every minute of it," Siobhán said smugly.

"That I do," Annie admitted with a contented sigh. "That I do."

D espite Annie's niggling worry, things went smoothly for the next few weeks. Annie had a spring in her step as she got up in the mornings, and she made good progress on her blog. Siobhán seemed content and happy as she painted. And they spent nearly every night together.

Today, Siobhán was out running errands and meeting with Gabriel at the gallery about some kind of summer art fair. The blog had launched that morning, and Annie had already been working for a few hours. She stood up from the chair in the kitchen and reached her arms as high overhead as she could while she stretched her back. She put on the kettle, then wandered around the apartment for a few moments to get her blood flowing while the water heated.

She'd always been a coffee drinker, but Siobhán had an extensive collection of teas, and Annie had really begun to enjoy drinking them. After the kettle whistled, Annie brewed the tea, then slowly walked through the apartment, waiting for the tea to cool to a drinkable temperature. She spotted her purse hanging on the hook by the door and her shoes stacked beside Siobhán's. In the bedroom, Siobhán had cleared a drawer and some closet space for her. She'd even installed another little shelf next to the sink just for Annie so she didn't have to keep hauling her toiletries back and forth.

Annie let out a small satisfied sigh at the sight of her things beginning to mingle with Siobhán's. It filled her with a sense of contentment, and she wondered if she should just move in officially. If not for the lingering worry that issues with Laura would crop up again, Annie probably wouldn't hesitate. But that had yet to fully dissipate. And she didn't want to be hasty.

As she meandered through the living room, Annie spotted the backs of several canvases propped against the wall on the far side of the room. She wondered if they were from some of the newer things Siobhán had done or if they were older works. She knew Siobhán kept a bunch of canvases in the large closet off the living room, although she'd never seen them up close. They were usually wrapped in cloth and carefully stored.

Annie flipped the first one over and studied it. It was of a woman, sprawled face down on the bed, her blonde hair spread out across the pillow. There was a voyeuristic, sexual feel to it that left Annie feeling flushed. Had Siobhán been painting her in her sleep?

The next piece made her pause for longer. It was also abstract, but something about it reminded Annie of two intertwined bodies. There was a splash of dark and another of gold in a sea of white. She smiled at the sight. It looked like Siobhán had painted them together. The same raw, sexual energy suffused the piece, and Annie felt her blood heat at the sight.

The next two were similar, although the face of the blonde was clearer. Annie tilted her head and studied the final one. It was her, but ... not. Something about it seemed off. Like looking in a slightly distorted mirror. The hair seemed longer too. She shrugged and set it down carefully. Siobhán was the artist. Nothing said she had to represent Annie exactly. Annie was probably reading way too much into some slashes of paint. How many times had she and Siobhán joked about people trying to read too much into art? A little bit of artistic license was to be expected.

Annie carefully returned the stack of paintings to their original spot, facing the wall. She assumed Siobhán was concerned about them getting bleached out and faded by the sun until she did whatever she was going to do with them.

Annie wondered why Siobhán hadn't shown any of the pieces to her. She'd shown Annie most of her paintings of Annie in the past. She felt a sudden stab of guilt, hoping she hadn't ruined some surprise Siobhán was planning. She'd feel terrible about that.

Annie was hard at work a few hours later when Siobhán returned. She rubbed Annie's shoulders for a minute, then bent down to press a kiss to the top of her hair. "How's it going?"

"Pretty well." Annie yawned, her jaw cracking a little. "The blog went live this morning, and we'll just have to wait and see. Traffic seems good so far, and there are a few comments. I'm trying to make sure I answer them promptly. Oh, and thanks for the marketing tips, by the way. I've never really had to use social media to promote my 'brand' before." She made a face.

"It's my least favorite part about being an artist, but you get used to it." Siobhán squeezed her shoulders. "I hope you know how proud of you I am. You've been working so hard. I know it's going to be a huge success."

"God, I hope so," Annie said fervently. "I don't know what I'll do if it's a flop."

"Well, we'll cross that bridge if we have to. For now, I want you to be positive about things."

"Yes, ma'am," Annie said teasingly. She closed the lid of her laptop. Now that everything was underway she could afford to take a little while to relax. "How was your day?"

"Good. The plans for the art fair are coming along. Some of the gallery staff will be manning the booths, but I think I'll stop by a few times. Mingle with people looking to buy."

"They'd be fools to not buy your work," Annie said. She thought of the paintings in the living room and frowned, wondering if she should say something to Siobhán about them or not. Nah, better not to, in case it was meant to be a surprise. "That's not for a few weeks though, isn't it?"

"No. I was just trying to figure out what to display. Gabriel's going to offer some limited edition prints at lower price points for people who might be impulse buying. I was trying to decide if I should paint a few small canvases for the fair as well. Quick, simple things I can dash off to have on hand."

"Can't hurt, right?"

"Exactly." Siobhán hummed. "Oh, Gabriel's doing some prints of your banner art, by the way. You should get some more business cards printed so I can put them near the prints. Maybe we can lure a few people to your blog that way."

"Clever idea." Annie smiled at her.

"I think we make a rather good team," Siobhán said with a smile.

"I do too," Annie said, reaching out to take Siobhán's hand. "I feel so lucky to have you in my life."

"Me too," Siobhán said softly. She frowned at Annie's mug. "Although … have you been breaking into my stash of tea again?"

Annie chuckled and stood to take the empty teapot and mug over to the sink to wash.

"I have."

"Cheeky." Siobhán grinned at her. "I guess I'll have to console myself that it wasn't my biscuits."

"Whatever happened to 'make yourself at home, Annie'? Or 'here's a key. I want you to move in'?"

Siobhán laughed. "All bets are off when it comes to tea and biscuits, you chancer." But she winked, and Annie knew she was just teasing.

"Good thing I'm not that big a fan of cookies," Annie said as she set the clean dishes on the counter

Siobhán rolled her eyes. "They're biscuits!"

"Cookies," Annie teased as she walked back to the table, knowing she could get a rise out of her girlfriend.

Siobhán grabbed Annie around the waist and tugged her onto her lap. "I love you so damn much, Annie Slocum," she muttered.

"I love you too." Annie shifted and cupped Siobhán's cheek in her hand. "I never thought I could be this happy."

Chapter Fifteen
October

"I need to run some canvases over to the gallery, then stop at the store." Annie looked up from the book she was reading to see Siobhán leaning over her. "I have an order placed for some supplies, and it just came in, so I'm going to take care of it all at once. Want me to pick up lunch on my way back?"

"Sure." Annie smiled up at her. Siobhán smiled back but it didn't quite reach her eyes. She'd seemed a little off in the last few days, and Annie wasn't sure why. "That sounds nice."

"Is there anything you'd like?"

"Hmm. The poppy seed chicken wraps from the deli around the corner?"

"I can do that." Siobhán kissed her briefly, then straightened. She lifted a nylon carrier onto her shoulder.

All morning, Siobhán had been fussing with the mysterious paintings that had been tucked in the corner of the living room for weeks, and now she was transporting them in a large carrier with a thick, nylon strap. Annie assumed she was taking them to the gallery for the upcoming art fair next week, but she hadn't specifically said anything about them to Annie.

"Do you need help with that?" Annie asked.

Siobhán shook her head. "I'm fine. I'll see you in a few hours." She disappeared around the corner, and Annie heard the door open.

"Love you!" Annie called out. But the door closed with no answer from Siobhán. Annie frowned. Odd. But maybe Siobhán hadn't heard her.

She tucked a bookmark into the book and set it on the ottoman beside Siobhán's laptop where she'd left it that morning. Siobhán had been up well

140

before Annie, although she hadn't been painting as usual. She'd just been sitting on the couch, staring at her laptop screen. When Annie had walked in, she'd looked startled and set her laptop down.

When Annie asked what was wrong, Siobhán had assured her it was just an issue with a potential client. But she'd seemed distracted and distant in the past few days, and Annie wondered if she should do something to surprise her.

It couldn't cost a lot of money—she was pretty broke at the moment with all the money she had put into getting the blog up and running—but maybe she could come up with something inexpensive. Siobhán was already going to pick up lunch, but maybe Annie could make dinner … no, maybe not dinner. Dessert? That would work. Siobhán loved dark chocolate, and now that she thought about it, it was the right time in Siobhán's cycle for her to be PMS-ing. Maybe that was why she'd seemed off lately. The obvious solution was a pan of extra-fudgy brownies.

Annie stood, grabbed her phone, and walked to the kitchen as she brought up her favorite brownie recipe. Once she was sure what she needed, she peered in the cupboards and refrigerator to see if Siobhán had all the ingredients on hand. She paused when she realized a photo was missing from the little collage on the freezer door; Siobhán had taken the clam digging photo down. She hadn't replaced it with anything, and the bare spot was glaringly obvious.

Annie stared at the blank space for a moment before she shrugged. Maybe Siobhán had decided she didn't need reminders of her past anymore. Annie smiled to herself at the thought and opened the refrigerator again to grab the butter and eggs. She'd bake the brownies for Siobhán now and surprise her when she got home. She couldn't wait to see Siobhán's face.

It didn't take Annie long to stir together melted butter and dark cocoa powder, then mix in the remaining ingredients. A short while later, she slid the pan into the pre-heated oven. She set a timer on her phone, then reached for the spatula. She licked it clean, smiling with pleasure at the thought of how much Siobhán would enjoy them. She wandered back to the living room, thinking about the rest of her day.

Hmm, what to do next? she wondered.

Work on the blog, probably, but unlike before, she didn't dread it. It was such a good feeling to actually look forward to her job.

141

Annie strode into Siobhán's bedroom to retrieve her laptop bag. She took it into the kitchen and set up at the little table by the window. It wasn't until she went to plug it in that she realized she'd forgotten to grab her laptop charger before she left her apartment.

"Damn it," she muttered. That was the bad part about going back and forth between the two places. She was always forgetting something important at one or the other. She kept a charger for her phone at Siobhán's but she hadn't gotten around to getting a second one for her laptop.

She powered up her computer anyway, figuring she could work for a while before it shut down, then groaned when she realized her battery was already dead. Unfortunately, Siobhán's charger was a completely different style and wouldn't help. She could do it on her phone, but it would take twice as long.

Hmm, Annie pondered. *What to do?* She brightened when she realized Siobhán's laptop was there. Surely Siobhán wouldn't mind her using her computer again. Annie could type up an outline of her ideas in a document and email it to herself from Siobhán's account. Easy enough.

She retrieved Siobhán's laptop from the living room and turned it on, her mind humming with ideas about what to tackle next.

The blog was doing well. Readership had been increasing steadily since the launch a few weeks ago, and Annie had contacted a few businesses that seemed interested in advertising. Next, she was going to look into networking with other bloggers to see if she could draw in traffic that way.

Intending to search for blogs to network with, she minimized the document and brought up the browser. It was open to Siobhán's email. Annie moved the cursor over the "new tab" option when two words sprang out at her. *Miss you,* they said.

That could be from her father, Annie argued with herself, trying not to give into the temptation to check. Although Annie knew Sean Murray and Siobhán had hardly spoken since Aileen Murray's death, so that was unlikely. *It could be a cousin or a friend she hasn't seen in a while,* she argued with herself. But against her better judgement, Annie's gaze returned to the text, unable to stop herself from reading just a few more lines.

> *It was great seeing you the other day, Siobhán. Lunch with you was … well, it made me think a lot about the time we spent together. I miss that. Miss you.*

> *You asked me if I was happy with Prescott, and I have been. But it's a different kind of happy. I have two beautiful children, a devoted husband, and*

the kind of life I've always wanted. But being with him isn't like being with you. It isn't crazy and passionate like when we were together. There's no nude modeling on the rooftop while my lover paints me. No nearly getting caught kissing in the fountain at City Square Park. No weekend marathons in bed that leave me so dehydrated I pass out.

I thought I was content, but you were right. I can never be completely happy with him. With any man. God, Siobhán, you made me crazy. Why did you let me go? Why didn't you stop me? Fight for me?

I thought I'd put things with you behind me, but imagine my surprise when I went to a party and saw one of your paintings hanging in the living room. I got so flushed, wondering what that stuffy crowd would think of the time we made love under the stars at the Outer Banks with my family a little ways down the beach.

I couldn't stop thinking about you after that, and I knew I had to see you again.

Annie's stomach dropped, and she swallowed hard. *Outer Banks? That has to be Laura.* Annie pressed her hand over her mouth as she continued reading, the words swimming in front of her watery eyes.

I know you said you were seeing someone, but if you still care about me the way I think you do, meet me at The Charles Hotel in Cambridge today at noon. Prescott thinks I'm visiting some friends from college. I'll be in room 532. Come straight up to the room, knock once, and I'll let you in.

Please, darling, I need to feel your touch again.

Always your muse,

-Laura

Tears finally spilled over and down her cheeks. Annie futilely wiped at them as a gut-wrenching sob escaped her.

No, no, no. This can't be happening. Siobhán wouldn't go behind my back. Siobhán loves me; she would never cheat on me, Annie thought.

But it was Laura. The one woman Siobhán had never gotten over. And the irrefutable proof was right in front of her. A sent message from Siobhán that said: *I'll be there.*

How could you do this to me, Siobhán? Annie thought, her heart aching. *I trusted you!*

She could hardly see the screen in front of her as she typed in the name listed in Siobhán's email along with a few keywords. It took almost no time to find the right Laura Caldwell and her politician husband, Prescott. Despite her blurry, tear-filled vision, she felt a cold sense of shock as she stared at the pictures of the woman on the screen.

Laura and Annie were so alike it was almost eerie. From the honey-blonde hair, to their blue eyes, to the shape of their jaws, they could have been sisters. Laura appeared to be a bit above average height for a woman—like Annie—and slender. Annie had an uncharitable thought that she'd probably age better than Laura since Laura had a deep summer tan.

But it was small comfort as she realized that Siobhán hadn't just been pining after Laura. She'd clearly been trying to replace her. Annie felt a sick lurch in her stomach as she thought about the paintings Siobhán had taken with her earlier today. *Are they a present for Laura?* Annie wondered. *Old memories of their time together?*

How could she have been so stupid, thinking that the paintings had been of her? They had been of Laura. Pictures from another time when Siobhán had everything she'd wanted.

A shrill sound startled Annie, and it took her a moment to realize it was the timer going off on her phone. She clumsily managed to turn it off. With tears streaming from her eyes, she turned off the hot oven and retrieved the brownies. She set them on the cutting board beside the sink, not caring when the pan slid off and clattered into the empty sink.

Annie sank to the floor, sliding down the cabinet front until she sat with her knees drawn up. She wrestled the bulky oven mitts off and threw them across the room where they smacked the recycling bin and made it rattle.

Annie put her head down and sobbed against her denim-clad knees, the moisture quickly soaking them.

Siobhán kissed me goodbye and ran off to be with Laura. The thought made her stomach churn. *Of course, when Laura contacted her, Siobhán went running,* Annie thought bitterly, *but why didn't she at least have the decency to end things first? Is she planning to fuck me and Laura at the same time?*

Annie had no idea how long she cried, but her stomach was cramped and her eyes felt tender and swollen by the time she heard the key in the door.

She lifted her head and wiped at her face, dreading the upcoming confrontation.

"I've brought lunch!" Siobhán called out. Annie heard the rustle of a bag, and Siobhán's voice sounded closer as she continued. "Is that something chocolate I smell? Oh, you are the most wonderful thing ever. I've been craving it all day. I nearly grabbed chocolate chip cookies at the deli, in fact, but I was trying to ... Annie?"

Annie glanced over at Siobhán as she stood in the kitchen doorway. *How can she look so innocent? Like nothing happened? How good a liar is she?* "I read the email from Laura," Annie said dully. "I wasn't trying to, but I accidentally left my charger at my place. I didn't think you'd mind if I used your laptop. I wasn't even snooping. You'd left the email open."

Siobhán gasped. "Oh, God, Annie ... I ..."

Annie stood, her legs so cramped from sitting in one position for so long she had to grab the edge of the counter to steady herself. But the pain from that didn't compare to the one in her heart. "You really met her for lunch a few days ago? Without telling me?"

Siobhán looked stricken, but she nodded yes.

Anger rose in her, bright and sharp. "How *could* you, Siobhán?" Annie lashed out. "You got jealous of my past with Gabriel, and yet you're the one sneaking behind my back to meet up with your ex-girlfriend. You're the one who clearly has no idea what she wants. You said you kept the photo of you clam digging because it was a reminder of a bad time in your life and something you never wanted to experience again. I think you've been lying to yourself—and to me—about what Laura still means to you! I noticed you took the photo off the fridge recently. Were you feeling too guilty every time you looked at it?" Annie spat. "Good! You should!"

Siobhán looked stricken. "Annie, no, I ... it's ..."

"No, I'm tired of it," Annie spat when Siobhán didn't continue. "I'm tired of feeling like some consolation prize. What am I to you? Laura's poor replacement?"

"You're not!" Siobhán burst out. "I swear, Annie. I don't love you because you remind me of Laura!"

145

"Guess it doesn't matter now, does it? God, how could you kiss me goodbye and go off to fuck her?" Annie gestured to the bag in Siobhán's hand. "And then come back to me with lunch? That's low. I *never* imagined you were that good a liar."

"I didn't!" Siobhán protested. She set down the bag and took a few steps toward Annie. But she held up her hand, and Siobhán stopped in her tracks. "I did kiss you goodbye. And I did take a few pieces that I'd been storing with me today. But I never had any intention of touching Laura." Tears spilled down Siobhán's cheeks. "Was I tempted? When she emailed me about my paintings, yeah, I was tempted for a moment. And then I saw her, and I realized it was the other way around. She was the poor imitation of *you*. You're strong, Annie. Strong enough to say what you want. *Who* you want. You're not afraid of who you are. But Laura? She is. She's a bleedin' coward."

"But you went to the hotel room."

"I did." Annie flinched. "Wait, Annie, listen. It wasn't for the reasons you think. I met Laura at the hotel, but I didn't fuck her. I didn't so much as touch her. I went to give her back the paintings I'd done of her and the two of us together. I wanted to wash my hands of them, start from scratch with you. I didn't go to make love to her, Annie, or win her back. I went because I needed to say goodbye and let her go. Finally find a sense of closure. Getting rid of those paintings was the last thing I needed to do to move on." She stared earnestly at Annie. "All I want, all I need—it's you."

Siobhán stepped a little closer. Annie tensed but didn't stop her.

"Why didn't you tell me? I don't understand that secrecy."

Siobhán frowned. "I knew how much my history with Laura bothered you. I thought … I thought it would be easier if I just got rid of her so we could move on." Siobhán was near tears. "I love you, Annie. I promise, I just wanted to get Laura out of my head and out of our lives."

"Were you going to tell me about any of it? Ever?"

Siobhán hesitated. "I—I don't know."

Annie shook her head, trying to deny that level of betrayal. "So you were just going to pretend like nothing ever happened?" she spat.

"I was afraid of losing you!"

Annie stared at her for a long moment, then shook her head. "I'm pretty sure you just did." She tried to push past Siobhán, who grabbed her arm.

"Please, *mo grá!*" Siobhán pleaded.

But Annie shook her off. "You don't get to call me that anymore. And you definitely don't get to call me your muse. Apparently, that's just something you call all of the women you sleep with."

"Feck," Siobhán swore. "Please, Annie, let's talk. Let me explain!"

Annie turned back to face her. "What is there to explain, Siobhán? I have given you so many chances, and I'm done. *We're* done."

She grabbed her purse off the hook by the door, slipped on her shoes, and was out the door before Siobhán could respond.

Chapter Sixteen

"**A**nnie?" Rebecca's knock jolted her out of a restless sleep. "Are you in there?"

"Yeah," she said groggily as she sat up. "I took a nap. You can open the door if you want though."

Rebecca poked her head inside. "Um, Siobhán is here. Well, not here in the apartment, but standing outside in the hallway. I told her to wait there. She brought by some of your stuff like your phone and laptop. She said you'd had a fight and left your stuff at her place."

"We did," Annie said dully.

"She said she wanted to talk, but I wasn't sure if that was what you wanted."

"I don't. Thanks for not letting her in." She met Rebecca's gaze.

Rebecca gave her a sympathetic look. "Oh, hun, you look awful."

"Thanks." Annie flopped back down.

"No, I just mean you look like you've been crying. I'll go get rid of Siobhán, then I'll bring you a cool cloth for your eyes. And I'm going to set your stuff down right here, okay?"

"K."

Annie stared up at the ceiling, listening to Rebecca's retreating footsteps, voices at the door, and then running water and Rebecca returning.

"Here you go." She passed a damp washcloth to Annie who obediently draped it over her closed eyes. It *did* help, actually. Her eyes were swollen and dry from falling asleep crying. The cool dampness was soothing. "Do you want to talk about it?"

"Not really."

The bed dipped beneath Rebecca's weight. "I'm really not trying to be nosy. I just want to help."

"I know." Annie was grateful. Rebecca hadn't always been her favorite person in the world, but she appreciated that she hadn't let Siobhán into the apartment. Annie sighed. "There's this woman Siobhán used to date. It didn't end well, and it turns out Siobhán never really got over her. She contacted Siobhán, they met for lunch, and the woman emailed to arrange a … hookup, I guess. Or to get back together. I don't fucking know which. I accidentally ran across the email."

"Oh, hun." Rebecca squeezed her calf. "That's awful."

"And the worst part is Siobhán didn't tell me about any of it. I mean, I knew about the ex but not about all the recent stuff. She claimed she just went to the hotel to give her some of the paintings she had done of her. I want to believe her, but she hid the whole thing from me. Lied to me about where she was going." Annie squeezed her eyes more tightly beneath the heavy washcloth. "How can I trust her after that?"

Rebecca was silent for a moment. "Maybe you just need a day or two to cool down, then you guys can talk more."

"I don't know." Annie pressed the cloth tighter to her face as if it would block out the truth along with the light in the room. "I'm not sure I even want to."

"Why?"

"I put up with all of her jealousy, her insecurity. I tried so hard to be *understanding* about the baggage she had with her ex. And then the minute that woman crooked her finger, Siobhán went running. Maybe she didn't cheat, but she still lied to me. She still hid things from me. I've bent over backward trying to be understanding. I don't think I can handle any more." Annie groaned when she realized she might have to face Siobhán again. "Fuck! Depending on how much she brought over, I may have to see her though. I have a ton of clothes and toiletries there."

"I think it's just your laptop and phone and stuff that she brought over. I didn't see any clothes."

"Fuck. Fuck. Fuck."

Rebecca patted her leg. "If it comes to that, I'll go get your stuff."

"You would do that?" Annie sat up, the washcloth falling onto her lap with a damp splat.

"Of course, I would." Rebecca gave her a small smile. "Trust me. I've been there. Well, not exactly, but I've had enough dudes lie and cheat on me to know when you just need someone else to deal with it."

"Thank you," Annie said sincerely. She leaned forward and hugged Rebecca.

"Of course, hun." Rebecca patted her shoulder a little awkwardly. They had been living together for two and a half years now, and this was the first time they'd ever hugged.

"I mean it." Annie sat back. "I couldn't stand the thought of facing her right now."

"Like I said, I've been there." Rebecca's smile was sympathetic. "Come on. You need to get your mind off things for the night. How about I make us something to eat, fix us some drinks, and we can watch TV together?"

"Sure," Annie agreed gratefully. She had no interest in eating bland, cardboard food and watching some stupid reality show, but it sure beat sitting alone in her room and crying.

When Annie staggered to bed later that night, she was exhausted, half-drunk, and feeling slightly sick. The distraction had been welcome though, and Annie was grateful to Rebecca for spending the evening with her.

Unfortunately, now that she was in bed, her mind wouldn't stop whirling with thoughts of Siobhán.

Her phone beeped quietly on the nightstand, and Annie rolled onto her side to grab it. She frowned when she saw there was a voicemail from Siobhán. A large part of her wanted to check the message and see what Siobhán had said, but she held down the power button until the phone went dark instead. What could Siobhán possibly say that would change Annie's mind?

Annie tossed the phone back on the nightstand and swore when it slid off onto the floor. She sighed heavily and decided she was too tired and too drunk to care.

She flopped onto her back again and stared at the ceiling. "What am I going to do about you, Siobhán?" she muttered.

Eventually, she fell into a restless sleep.

When she finally crawled out of bed the next morning, after tossing and turning all night, she realized she'd never been gladder she didn't have a normal 9 to 5 job to go to. There was no way she could have made it.

She staggered to the bathroom and winced when she saw her reflection in the mirror. Her hair was a mess, she'd forgotten to wash her makeup off before bed, and her head throbbed because she'd ignored Rebecca's warnings to drink plenty of water.

She did the best she could to pull herself together, but as she walked toward the kitchen, she sent up a silent prayer that no one else would be home. Of course, Trent was sitting in the kitchen eating a bowl of cereal. He nodded at her.

"Sorry things went bad with your girl. She seemed nice." His voice was a little gruff, but it was much kinder than usual.

Annie swallowed hard and nodded. "Uh, thanks."

Thankfully, he didn't say anything else, and she was able to guzzle several glasses of water and make a cup of coffee in peace. She returned to her bedroom, made the bed, and then sat on it, wondering what she should do with herself. She wasn't really in the mood to work on the blog, but she didn't have much choice. The world wasn't going to stop just because she'd gotten her heart broken.

Oh, God, why had she ever created the blog? It was Siobhán's brainchild and Siobhán's painting would stare her in the face every time she logged on. Every time she saw an ad for the Quinn Gallery, she'd be reminded of her relationship with Siobhán and how they'd met. How Siobhán had broken her heart.

It was the first career she'd been truly excited about, and now it would be never-ending torture.

"No," Annie muttered. "I'm not letting you take that from me too, Siobhán. That's *my* blog. You don't get to ruin it for me."

It was easier said than done, of course, but she felt a sense of determination wash over her. She wiped at her eyes and reached for the laptop bag.

It was either work or mope about Siobhán. Only one of them would accomplish something productive. Siobhán had broken her heart. Annie wasn't about to let her take her new career too.

She would be a success despite her. She'd just have to learn to live with the reminders somehow.

When Annie pulled her laptop out of the bag, a letter fluttered to the bed. She picked it up with a feeling of trepidation. She handled it gingerly, as if it might spontaneously combust at any moment. Or maybe that was just her heart that was in danger of that.

She had to take a deep breath before she steeled her spine and began to read.

I'm sorry, Annie. I made a huge mistake. I realize that now. The minute Laura contacted me, I should have told you.

And I never should have met her at the hotel. I don't know why I did that. I went with the best of intentions but maybe I wanted her to think for a minute that I was there for her. Maybe I wanted to hurt her as much as she hurt me. But you're the one who ended up getting hurt, and I'll never forgive myself for that. You deserve better.

And I don't know that there's any way I can get you to forgive me or earn your trust again, but I will do whatever it takes. I love you, Annie, and I can't imagine my life without you.

The letter was short and to the point, but by the time Annie finished reading, tears were streaming down her cheeks. She wiped them away and sat back against the headboard, closing her eyes for a moment, her determination to cut Siobhán out of her life and move on wavering.

She was still angry at Siobhán. So fucking angry. Her heart still felt like it had been stomped on. But she was starting to think she might have to face Siobhán at least one more time.

She was afraid if she walked away from Siobhán without talking to her, she'd never get over her.

Annie had seen what unresolved feelings had done to Siobhán. Even if Annie never forgave Siobhán, maybe it was better for her to confront her, clear the air, and then move forward. Because if she didn't, she was afraid she'd wind up regretting it.

"Better to get it over with, I guess," she muttered quietly to herself. "You can fall apart after."

Annie got up, dressed in the first clothes she could lay her hands on, and did little more than scrub her teeth and run a brush through her hair again. What did it matter how she looked?

She ran into Rebecca on her way out. "Hey, how are you doing?" she said softly.

Annie swallowed. "I'm okay."

Rebecca's gaze swept over her. "You heading out?"

"Yeah."

"Are you going to see her?"

Annie nodded. "I don't know what will happen, but I want to talk to her. At the very least, maybe I can get some closure and get my stuff from her place."

Rebecca frowned, and for a moment, Annie thought she was going to try to talk her out of it. Or comment on her un-made up appearance. "Well, good luck," she said instead. "Let me know how it goes. I'm here if you wanna talk."

"Thanks," Annie said gratefully. "I know we're not super close, but you've been really great."

"Hey, we girls have to stick together," Rebecca said. "Just so you know; my favorite ice cream is Death By Chocolate, so you may want to have some on hand for when it's my turn."

"That's a pretty cynical view of relationships," Annie pointed out.

"Yeah, I know." Rebecca sighed. "I've just dated enough douchebags to know that's how it goes. I was starting to think maybe you were onto something with the lesbian thing, but I guess not."

Annie managed a faint smile. "I don't think any gender has a monopoly on being a jerk. I'd just gotten out of a relationship with a guy when I moved in here."

"Yeah, fair enough," Rebecca said. "I mean it though. I'm here for you."

"Thanks. I don't have a lot of close friends, so that's really nice."

"Of course. Uh, look, I hate to cut this short but I've gotta run or I'll be late for work." She sounded apologetic.

"Oh, sorry." Annie stepped back. "Go. I'll let you know what happens with—with Siobhán." It was painful to say her name. God, could she really cut Siobhán out of her life completely? She couldn't imagine it. But she couldn't imagine what Siobhán would say that would make Annie forgive her either.

"Thanks." Rebecca grabbed her purse off the bench by the door. "See ya."

Annie put on her shoes and followed more slowly, torn between reluctance to face Siobhán and a need to get this over with. Whatever *this* was. She'd been fully convinced there was nothing Siobhán could say that would make her change her mind about breaking up. But now, Annie was less sure of that. And even less sure of whether or not she wanted Siobhán to succeed.

Chapter Seventeen

Annie had to take several deep breaths before she could knock on Siobhán's door. Siobhán opened it a minute later.

Annie felt a guilty stab of satisfaction at her messy, unwashed hair, the dark circles under her eyes, and the blue T-shirt Annie recognized as her own. She wore it with a pair of yoga pants and a thick, warm-looking sweater Annie knew she'd brought back from Ireland on her last trip home.

A part of her was glad Siobhán looked wrecked, but the other part of her wanted to pull Siobhán into her arms and make the hurt go away. God that was fucked up.

"Annie," Siobhán said hoarsely. "I …"

"Can I come in?" Annie asked quietly.

"Yeah. Of course." Siobhán opened the door wider and stepped back. Siobhán shut the door after her, and they stood there in silence for a moment.

"How are you?" Siobhán finally asked.

Annie laughed hollowly. "I'm not great. I've been thinking about things pretty much nonstop since I left yesterday. Thanks for bringing some of my stuff by though. I really needed my phone and laptop."

"Yeah, I know." Siobhán looked down. "I thought about bringing your clothes too, but I—I wanted there to be a reason you came back here."

"I didn't come for my stuff," Annie admitted.

Siobhán lifted her head. "No?"

"No. I don't know what I want to say or what I want the outcome to be, but I came here to talk."

Siobhán burst into tears. She hastily wiped at her eyes. "Sorry, sorry. I'm not trying to make you feel bad for me. I fucked up, and I know it's all my fault, but God, the thought that maybe there's even the smallest chance I could fix it …" She wiped at the tears again.

"I know." For as angry and emotional as Annie had been yesterday, at the moment, she felt strangely calm.

"Would you like a cuppa?"

"Sure," Annie agreed. She was pretty sure if she and Siobhán were truly over, it would be the last cup of tea she would ever drink.

She followed Siobhán into the kitchen and winced when she thought about the fight that had happened in there the day before. But there weren't any places they could go in the apartment that weren't filled with memories of her and Siobhán. They'd made love on the couch, in the bedroom, the bathroom, even here in the kitchen. They'd kissed everywhere, held hands, talked of a future together.

The memories felt like ghosts, filling up the space around them. She took a seat at the table anyway as Siobhán filled the kettle.

Annie's gaze passed over the refrigerator and saw the blank spot where the photo was missing again. It made her wonder how many other ghosts lingered here. "Did Laura ever live here?" she blurted out.

Siobhán lifted her head, her eyes wide. She set the kettle onto the burner with a thunk. "No, why?"

"I—I just wondered."

"No, I moved here after she and I broke up. Laura has never even been here."

"Oh. Okay." Annie felt weirdly relieved.

Siobhán's lips tightened briefly as if she was about to say something, but instead, she twisted the knob on the stove and lit the burner.

It wasn't until they had cups of tea in front of them that either of them spoke again.

"Can I say something, Annie?" She nodded. "I'm sorry. I'm so fecking sorry."

"I know," Annie admitted. "I read your note. And I believe that you are sorry and that you know you fucked up. But how can I trust you?"

Siobhán looked at her with watery eyes. "I don't know."

"I can't get the image out of my head of you kissing her. Going to her hotel room and making love to her," Annie confessed.

"I didn't, Annie. She tried to kiss me, and I pulled back," Siobhán protested. "We never touched each other. I swear it."

"I know. I—I believe that. But it doesn't stop the images in my head." Annie looked up at the ceiling, blinking back tears. "I made the mistake of finding Laura online."

"How did you manage that?"

"I saw her last name in her email. Looked it up in conjunction with the keywords politician and Boston. I was an investigative reporter, Siobhán. She wasn't hard to find." Annie swallowed. "But I wish I hadn't. I didn't need to know that she was thin and blonde and that we look enough alike we could be mistaken for sisters."

"Annie ..." Siobhán said, her tone anguished.

"No, that part's my own fault. You know what they say about curiosity and the cat." She took a deep breath. "But when it comes down to it, that's what hurts most. That you were trying to replace her. I don't want to be her replacement."

"You're *not*," Siobhán protested.

"It looks that way from this end. I look like her. I saw the paintings you had stacked against the wall a few weeks ago. I peeked at them and thought they were of me." Annie blinked back tears. "But they weren't, were they?"

Siobhán shook her head.

Annie felt sick seeing it confirmed. "They were Laura. Ones you painted of her. Ones of the two of you together."

Siobhán merely nodded, as if Annie's questions had rendered her mute.

"I looked at them, and I knew something was a little off. They didn't seem quite like me, but I wanted to believe they were." Annie's voice cracked. "I wanted to trust you, Siobhán."

Siobhán closed her eyes, a single track of tears leaking down her left cheek.

"Laura was your muse first; the woman you wanted to spend your life with. She was the one you've loved longest. How can I compete?"

"I know it looks like that, but that isn't what this is. I swear it."

"Tell me how," Annie said, tears streaming down her cheeks too. "Tell me how I can *ever* believe I am special to you after this."

"Oh, Annie." Siobhán burst into tears again. She got up from the chair and dropped to her knees in front of Annie. Too shocked to respond, Annie let Siobhán take her hands as she looked up at Annie. "That's how I am in a relationship. I fall in love, and I'm filled with ideas, with inspiration. I can't change that."

"Oh." Annie felt strangely deflated, hurt and disappointed that she hadn't been unique.

"I never meant to mislead you."

"I know," Annie admitted. "You never claimed I was the only one. I just assumed …"

Siobhán looked miserable. "I love you. And you *do* inspire my work. I'm filled with ideas when I touch you. Every day I'm with you makes me more creative, more inspired to make art. With you, I've been pushing my boundaries, making the kind of art I've only dreamed of in the past."

"More than with Laura?" Annie felt petty even asking, but she needed to know.

"Yes."

"You're not just saying that to make me feel better?"

Siobhán shook her head. "I love you in a way I never loved Laura. I was infatuated with her, obsessed with her, but what we had was never real. We were never building a future *together*. It was all one-sided because she couldn't admit to her family or even to herself who she is."

158

"But that doesn't change *your* feelings for Laura," Annie said gently. "Just because Laura was conflicted about her identity doesn't mean you loved her any less than you thought you did at the time. It only means Laura didn't feel the same for you. Or wasn't able to admit it."

"But if she never intended to be with me—like we talked about—it wasn't real. If she always knew, eventually, she'd give in and do what they wanted, then the things she said about our future meant nothing."

Annie frowned. "Maybe. Or maybe she wanted so badly to believe it, she convinced herself. You'll never know. She may not even know."

"I suppose," Siobhán muttered. "But what does it matter, Annie? It doesn't matter what Laura is or what she believed at the time. It doesn't even matter what she wants now. Even if she had promised me everything I ever wanted to hear, I wouldn't have gotten back together with her."

"Because she would still be hiding her sexuality?"

"No! Because of you. Even if Laura divorced her husband and took out a full page ad in The Boston Globe telling the world she's a lesbian, I wouldn't date her again," Siobhán said scornfully. "It's because Laura isn't the woman I'm in love with. The feelings I thought I had for her are long gone. All I had to do was sit across a table from her to realize it. I thought I was still hung up on her, but I was wrong."

Tears rolled down Siobhán's cheeks again, and the sight tugged at Annie's heart.

"I love *you*, Annie. And I will do anything to win you back. I can't bear the thought of losing you."

"I don't like it either," Annie admitted. "But while I might be able to forgive you, I don't know that I can ever forget, Siobhán."

"I know. Can I say one more thing?"

"You can say whatever you want," Annie said. She couldn't promise it would change anything, but there was no reason not to let Siobhán say her piece.

"Part of the reason I went to see Laura was because I knew I needed to put things to rest with her. I returned the paintings and told her to do what she wanted with them. Burn them, if necessary. Laura was a ghost we needed to be rid of. And I know I went about it the wrong way, and I may have risked everything that matters to me to do it, but it worked. I did manage to exorcise her. My feelings for her are dead and buried. I just knew we couldn't move forward if this was hanging over us in the future. You said that yourself."

Annie bristled at the idea that somehow this had been her fault. "That doesn't excuse anything, Siobhán. I never told you to meet Laura for lunch or go to her hotel room."

"I know." Tears spilled down Siobhán's cheeks again. "But how else was I supposed to get closure?"

"I don't know!" Annie threw up her hands. "But we could have figured it out together! Maybe you could have come to me, said that Laura had contacted you, and asked how I felt about you meeting her. Or something. I don't know. I just know there had to be a way of going about it that didn't involve sneaking around behind my back."

"You wouldn't have been upset by that? By learning Laura had contacted me and that I wanted to meet with her?"

"I probably would have been upset," Annie admitted. "But less upset than I am right now, that's for sure. Tell me why you hid it from me. I don't understand."

"Because I knew how much I'd already asked you to deal with. You'd put up with my jealousy, my past with Laura coming up constantly …" Siobhán swallowed audibly. "And I was terrified that if I asked for more, it would be too much. And I was ashamed that my heart raced when I saw the first message from Laura. And that thinking about her made me doubt my feelings for you. Just for a moment, but …"

Annie squeezed her eyes shut as tears leaked from the corners. Siobhán had been right about one thing, hearing that was difficult. It hurt. But not as much as it hurt knowing that Siobhán had met with Laura behind her back. She opened her eyes and wiped at them. "I understand that, Siobhán. I do, but it's no excuse. Yes, it would have hurt to hear that, but at least, it would have been honest. And I would have, at least, felt like we were in this together instead of me against you and Laura like always."

Siobhán looked anguished. "I never meant for you to feel that way, Annie."

"I know you didn't." Annie felt like a suddenly deflated balloon as the anger leeched out of her. "But I do. And I'm tired of it."

Siobhán gripped her hands. "How can I make this right?"

"I don't know, Siobhán." Annie shook her head. "I really have no idea."

"I wish I knew what to do, Annie."

"Me too." Annie sighed, and they were both silent for a few moments. "Tell me one thing."

"Of course; anything."

"Are you really over her now? For good? *If* we can move forward, is this the end of Laura being a part of our lives?"

"Yes." Siobhán's answer was so swift and matter of fact that Annie blinked. Despite her doubts about Siobhán's trustworthiness, strangely enough, she believed Siobhán about that.

"No more ghosts? No more doubts about my sexuality or my need for anyone but you?"

"None. Not a shred of doubt. And I swear to you, Annie, Laura is in the past now. She'll have no place here. "

Annie sighed. "I hope so. Because this is it. No more. I can't do it. The smallest hint of it and I'm done."

"I know, Annie," Siobhán said gravely.

Annie wet her lips. "Can you give me a few minutes to think? Alone?"

Siobhán nodded. "I'll go in the other room. Take all the time you need."

"Thanks."

Siobhán left the kitchen, closing the French doors behind her. Annie stared down at her half-empty tea cup as she considered the past few months with Siobhán.

Their relationship had been tumultuous. There was no denying that. The highs were higher than anyone Annie had ever been with. But the lows were lower. She didn't like Siobhán's jealousy. She hated Laura's presence in Siobhán's past. And she detested the lies.

But despite everything, Annie believed Siobhán *could* change. Since their fight at the gallery, Siobhán had reined in her jealousy. Siobhán now seemed

161

sincere about being over Laura, so Annie could hope that in the future, that wouldn't be an issue again.

But the lies made her pause. Could she trust Siobhán again? That was the part that terrified her.

Annie weighed all of it. The fights. The making love. The fears and worries. The love and support. The good and the bad.

As she weighed them all, the scales tipped in favor of Siobhán being in her life. If Siobhán had really let Laura go, maybe it was worth giving their relationship another shot.

Annie was scared shitless. Her head told her it would take hard work to get to a point where she could trust Siobhán again. And she was risking getting her heart broken again. But her heart told her that Siobhán was worth it. Their relationship was worth it.

A thousand emotions swirled through her as she stood on shaky legs and walked to the door. A part of her wondered if she should just cut her losses and run, but something still tugged her toward Siobhán, who sat on the loveseat with her legs drawn up, her chin on her knees. She seemed to be staring blankly at the cushion a few feet away. She looked small and lost, and the sight of her made Annie's heart ache with hurt and love.

"Siobhán?" Annie said quietly.

She lifted her head, her eyes wide and startled-looking. Her lips trembled for a moment before she pressed them tightly together. "Yeah?" Her voice sounded hoarse.

"I've had some time to think."

Siobhán drew in a deep, shuddering breath and stood. She squared her shoulders as she looked at Annie like she was about to face a firing squad.

"C'mere," Annie said softly.

Siobhán skirted around the loveseat and came to stand a few feet from Annie. For a moment, Annie just looked at her. There was no trace of the beautiful, self-assured woman Annie had first met. Or of the gorgeous, sexy one who'd seduced her during their first date. Not the soft, sweet girlfriend who curled up against Annie in her sleep. Or the strong, encouraging partner Annie had begun to build a life with.

Now she was a stripped-down version of the woman Annie had fallen in love with: devastated, raw, heartbroken. Remorseful.

Annie could smell the sharp scent of acrylic paints in the air and the faint milk and honey sweetness that always clung to Siobhán's skin. It made her heart ache, and she felt a sense of surety settle over her. There was no way she could walk out the door and never see Siobhán again.

It was terrifying, giving Siobhán the chance to hurt her all over again, but Annie knew deep down in her gut, it was the right choice.

Annie managed a faint smile.

"I'm really scared to get my heart broken again, but I love you, Siobhán," she said softly. "And if you're sure this is the last time Laura will intrude on our relationship, I'm willing to give this another shot."

Siobhán gave Annie a faint, tremulous smile back. "You mean that?"

"Yes. I'm fucking scared, Siobhán. I know I can't handle another fight like this and if you lie to me again, it's over, but I'm not ready to give up on us yet."

Before Annie could blink, she felt Siobhán's body against hers. She clung to Annie, her arms iron-strong around Annie's shoulders. "I hated myself for hurting you. I could never have forgiven myself losing you," Siobhán said in a choked voice. "I've missed you, *mo grá*."

Annie stroked her hand down Siobhán's spine. "I know."

"I can't lose you, Annie. Not because you inspire my work or because I just need to be with *someone*. And not because you're like anyone but you. I can't lose you because I love you. And I've never loved anyone as much as I love you."

Annie felt tears leak from the corners of her eyes as she pressed her lips against Siobhán's. The taste of Siobhán's lips on her own was the sweetest thing she'd tasted in a long time. "I love you too. So much."

Siobhán stroked a finger down Annie's cheek, wiping away the moisture. "I know it'll take time, but I will be sure you can trust me again. I swear it."

"I believe that."

Siobhán offered her a tremulous smile and took her hand. Wordlessly, Annie followed her down the hall to the bedroom. Siobhán undressed her, and then herself. When they slid into bed naked, it didn't feel like the precursor to the angry, lustful sex they'd had before.

This felt different. And maybe that was good. Maybe they were growing as a couple.

Siobhán gripped her tightly, but as her hands roamed across Annie's back, they weren't seeking anything but reassurance. It was enough for Annie to give it back.

Chapter Eighteen

December

"Do you have plans tonight?" Annie asked her roommate.

Rebecca shook her head. "No. What's up?"

"I was wondering if you'd be up for a girl's night. I could use some advice. Oh, and Dee'll be home. I talked to her already. Trent's at a bachelor party for some friend of his, so I thought maybe the three of us could hang out."

"Sure." Rebecca brightened. "That sounds fun. Want me to take care of dinner?"

"No offense, Rebecca, but your meals kinda suck."

She laughed. "Oh, thanks, Annie."

"Oh, come on, it can't possibly taste that good to you."

Rebecca shrugged. "I know some people are way into food, but I really don't care. It's just fuel to me."

"Well, I'd like to enjoy what I'm eating, so I've got food covered. I'll order something in. Any requests?"

Rebecca shrugged. "Nah, I don't care. I'll call this my cheat day. Want me to whip up some drinks?"

"That sounds great." Annie smiled at her. "Thanks."

"It'll be fun!"

A few hours later, the three of them were curled up on the couches in the living room. Rebecca had made pitchers of ginger pear punch, and Annie was already feeling slightly buzzed.

"What exactly did you put in this?" she asked, peering down at her glass.

Rebecca snickered. "Brandy. Lots and lots of brandy."

"Why didn't we do this before?" Annie asked. "This is fun."

Dee snorted. "Because I work all the damn time, Rebecca was always with some man, and you were a stuck-up bitch."

"Oh, that." Annie nodded. "Yeah, that sounds about right."

Rebecca let out a peal of laughter. "At least, you admit it."

"I kinda was." She shrugged. "I don't like it, but there's nothing much I can do about that now."

"Nah, you're cool," Dee said. "So what did you want to talk about anyway?"

Annie looked down at her glass. "I'm thinking about moving in with Siobhán."

"Damn! Are you ready for that?"

"I don't know," Annie admitted. "I think so. I'm just scared."

"Why?" Rebecca angled herself so she was facing Annie and crossed her legs.

"I don't know. I've been burned before. The whole reason I moved in here was because I got screwed over when Mark and I broke up."

Rebecca shrugged. "Isn't that always the risk with any relationship?"

"Yeah. I don't know. I'm probably overthinking things."

"No, you have a point," Dee said. "You and Siobhán went through some rough stuff, and you want to be sure you're not going to end up in a bad place again. I get that. You're protecting yourself; that's smart."

"I don't agree," Rebecca said. "I think Annie's just scared."

"Of course, I'm scared. God, Siobhán nearly broke my heart. I'm not sure I want to do that again," Annie pointed out.

It had been two months since *The Laura Incident*—as Annie had taken to calling it in her mind—and she was gradually beginning to let go of her wariness. But, it had taken time.

"Of course not. Who wants to get their heart broken?" Dee turned a look on Annie. "Does Siobhán love you?"

"Yes," Annie said without hesitation.

"Do you love her?"

"Yes."

"Do you think she wants what's best for you?"

Annie thought for a moment. "Yeah, I really do."

"Then you have to let go of all those doubts. Because it isn't going to protect you from getting hurt. It's just gonna keep you two from moving forward."

"Huh. That's a good point," Rebecca said. She looked over at Annie. "We all know I'm a hot mess when it comes to relationships. You should probably listen to Dee."

"I'm not sure that's such a good idea. I don't know what I'm doing either."

Rebecca frowned at her. "What are you talking about, Dee? You've been with Trent forever."

"And I think it's about over. I don't know."

"Really?" Annie asked. "You guys seem pretty happy."

"I'm pretty sure he's thinking about proposing." Dee sighed, but it wasn't one of happiness. She sounded resigned. "He's definitely been hinting at it."

"Shouldn't that be a good thing?" Rebecca said.

"It should, right?" Dee looked over at her. "But I don't feel excited about it. I'm more excited about my degree, you know?"

"To be fair, a nursing degree is a way bigger accomplishment than marrying Trent," Rebecca said.

BRIGHAM VAUGHN

Dee laughed. "Yeah, I've worked my damn ass off for the degree." She shrugged. "Maybe that's the problem with Trent."

"What? Because you never had to work at it with him?"

"Yeah, kinda. He's just ..." Dee seemed like she was struggling for words. "He tries so hard to be tougher than he is no matter how many times I tell him that's not the kind of guy I want. He couldn't even admit to Annie that he likes to eat pussy. Who wants a man like that?"

"It was weird," Annie admitted.

"I'm torn because he's not a bad guy despite all his bullshit. And being with Trent was great while I was in school. He cares about me. I never doubted that. The problem is he's comfortable, but he's not exciting. I want more than that. I want someone who challenges me."

"Yeah, I understand that," Annie said. Siobhán did challenge her. And when she thought about a future with Siobhán, she was sure it would always be interesting.

"Plus, I'm graduating in December, and I'm thinking about leaving Boston," Dee continued. Rebecca let out a soft sound of surprise. "Do I really want to drag a husband along with me wherever I go? I'm not sure I do. I love him, but I can live without him, you know?"

"Yeah, I see your point," Annie said.

"Wait. So you're both going to leave me?" Rebecca said. "What the hell?"

"Sorry, girl." Dee offered Rebecca a small smile. "But I'm not letting anything get in the way of me living my dream."

"Oh, sure, you and Annie leave me, and I'm left with a heartbroken Trent. You guys suck." Rebecca crossed her arms and pouted.

Annie laughed. "Hey, I haven't decided anything yet."

"Yeah, but you will." Rebecca sounded confident. "You and Siobhán will move in together, you'll write your blog, she'll paint, and then someday you'll have a beautiful lesbian wedding and babies together."

Annie laughed. But a small part of her thought that the future Rebecca predicted sounded pretty damn good. Was it that easy though? Could she really just move in with Siobhán and move on to build a future together? What if she failed? What if they failed?

And what if they succeeded?

Sure, she had a lot to lose. But she had so much to gain. There was always the possibility that she'd regret choosing to move forward toward a future with Siobhán. But she knew if she didn't try, she'd regret that for sure.

"Yeah, maybe you're right," Annie said softly. She took a deep breath and looked at the women across the room. "Okay. I'm going to do it. I'm going to move in with Siobhán."

Dee gave her an encouraging smile, and Rebecca let out an excited squeal as she came over to hug Annie. It occurred to Annie that Rebecca was right. They were all going in different directions now.

"Ugh, why is it that now I feel like we've gotten to be good friends just as I'm leaving," Annie said, surprised by how sad she felt at the thought.

"Just because you move out doesn't mean we can't stay friends, silly." Rebecca hugged her again. "We're not going anywhere."

"I might be," Dee said.

"Damn it, Dee; I was trying to make Annie feel better, not worse," Rebecca said.

That struck Annie as one of the funniest things she'd heard, and it wasn't until she splashed punch on the floor that she realized it was probably because she was rather tipsy.

She let out a small laugh and set the glass down before she stood.

"Where are you going?" Rebecca asked.

"To call my girlfriend and ask her if she wants to move in together," Annie said with a smile.

"Aww, that's sweet. But I thought we were hanging out tonight! What happened to hoes before bros," Rebecca called after her.

"I don't think that works with lesbians, honey," Dee said.

"Hoes before hoes?" Rebecca yelled. Annie shook her head as she walked down the hall, weaving a little from the effect of the brandy.

"I think you better quit while you're ahead," she heard Dee say with a snort.

Annie was still smiling as she closed the bedroom door behind her and flopped onto the bed, immediately reaching for her phone.

"What happened to girls' night?" Siobhán said as she answered.

"I'm drunk." Annie reconsidered. "Well, tipsy anyway. It was fun though. I'm going to miss Dee and Rebecca."

"Why? Are they moving?"

"No," Annie said. "Sort of. Dee is. But that's not the point. I was kind of hoping *I* might be."

There was silence on the other end for a moment. "Are you saying what I think you are?" Siobhán finally said. There was a hesitant, hopeful note in her voice.

"Yeah, I am. Do you want to move in together, Siobhán?" Annie asked. "Because I really want to start a future with you. I know I'm drunk-ish and that probably isn't the best time to make these decisions, but I promise, I want this. I'm sure of that. So what do you say? Should we move in together? Plan a future together?"

"*Mo grás,*" Siobhán said, the words a hushed, reverent whisper. "Oh, yes, Annie. I've been ready. I've just been waiting for you to ask."

Chapter Nineteen
June

Annie sighed as strong fingers dug into the muscles of her shoulders. Siobhán's sweet scent surrounded her. "Mmm, hello."

"Hello." Siobhán sounded like she was smiling. "How's the work going?"

"Good." Annie let her head fall forward as Siobhán worked her way up Annie's neck. "Better now."

"I should hope so." She could hear the smile in Siobhán's voice. "Tell me about your day."

"Oh, I spoke with someone at a whale watching company who's interesting in being a featured company on the blog."

"Are you considering it?"

"Possibly." Annie moaned when Siobhán hit a particularly sore spot at the base of her skull. "Oh, yes, right there."

"Pros?"

"Good money. The company seems good, or at least the contact person I've been dealing with does."

"Cons?"

"None that I can see so far. But, I'll want to research the company more. And we'll have to take a whale watching trip."

"Oh, no," Siobhán said. "How horrible. You really ask the worst things of me, Annie."

Annie stuck out her tongue, even though Siobhán couldn't see it. "How do you stand it?"

"Oh, I don't know." Siobhán leaned in and spoke in Annie's ear. "Maybe it's all the orgasms you repay me with."

"It could be that," Annie agreed with a smile.

Siobhán lifted her hands and stepped away. Annie swiveled in her chair and looked up at her. "How'd the meeting with the auction winners go?"

"Wonderful!" Siobhán beamed. "The couple was delighted with the painting and, of course, Gabriel is salivating over the thought of the commission he's getting."

"I'm sure he is." Annie rolled her eyes, but it was out of habit rather than real annoyance. Gabriel had been a huge contributor to the success of her blog. And the painting Siobhán was referring to was the Boston skyline piece she'd created for Annie's blog. They'd auctioned it off as part of a charity auction, which had led to a flood of traffic. It had been a boon for everyone, including the local women's center they would be donating the proceeds to.

"What do you have planned for the rest of the day?" Siobhán asked.

"Answering emails, writing blog posts, and updating expenses in my budgeting software."

"All in a day of the life of a successful blogger!" Siobhán said.

"Yes," Annie agreed. Her blog had been remarkably successful in a short time. She'd been astonished by the companies that had reached out to her once it was up and running, and while she wasn't likely to grow rich on it anytime soon, it had been voted in the Top 10 for new blogs on the Boston A-List website. It paid the bills. And most importantly, Annie loved her work.

"What do you think about whale watching on Friday?"

"Sounds lovely. And who knows? Maybe it'll spark some new ideas for me."

Annie frowned at her. "Still struggling?"

Siobhán sighed. "Unfortunately."

The one blemish in their otherwise wonderful life together had been that Siobhán had been struggling with her creativity since *The Laura Incident*. The flood of ideas she'd had slowed to a trickle, and she'd repainted more canvases than she'd completed. Even the ones she'd done, she hadn't been happy with.

It broke Annie's heart every time she walked into their office and saw Siobhán staring at a blank canvas with a deep furrow over her brow.

When Annie had expressed her worries that she or their relationship had somehow caused the creative block, Siobhán had assured her it had nothing to do with her. But whatever the cause, Annie hated to see the person she loved struggling.

Thankfully, Siobhán still had money coming in. The sale of her completed paintings from her last show had allowed them to put a little into savings and to move from Siobhán's one-bedroom apartment into a roomier two-bedroom a floor above in the same building. They'd used the second bedroom as a combined studio for Siobhán and office for Annie. She often found herself sitting and staring around the space, smiling at the sight of their mingled passions.

The rest of the apartment had slowly come together as well. Annie had been delighted to realize that their new bedroom was shaded by the large, sturdy tree in front of the building, much like her room at the apartment with Dee, Trent, and Rebecca, and it gave her the same tranquil feeling.

"Everything okay, *mo grá?*" Siobhán asked, and Annie started.

"Yes. Sorry. I got lost in thought. Did I tell you Rebecca and Trent are dating?

Siobhán blinked at her. "Really?"

"Apparently. I guess the woman who moved in after Dee left—the one who took my old bedroom—was flirting with Trent, Rebecca got jealous, and one thing led to another. I don't know. I'm baffled, but maybe it'll make more sense after I talk to Rebecca. We're grabbing a drink after she gets out of work."

"I can't decide if that's a brilliant pairing or horrifying," Siobhán said.

Annie agreed. "I'm inclined to think the latter, but we'll see. I'll let you know the details when I get home tomorrow. I'm combining drinks out with a review I've been meaning to do of the new bar that opened down the street."

Siobhán laughed. "You can take a day off here and there, you know?"

"I know," Annie said with a sigh. "But now that I'm enjoying what I'm doing, sometimes it's hard to turn it off."

Siobhán smiled faintly. "I remember that."

The note of wistfulness in her voice made Annie's heart ache, and she stood and went over to Siobhán. "I'm sorry things aren't coming together for you right now."

Siobhán shrugged and let out a quiet sigh. "As am I. But knowing I have you makes it easier. We'll get through it."

"Of course, we will." Annie smoothed Siobhán's dark hair away from her face. "I love you."

"I love you too." Siobhán pulled her closer and brushed her lips across Annie's. "More than you can possibly imagine."

Annie closed her eyes and deepened the kiss. Living together had done nothing to blunt their passion for each other, and she couldn't count the number of times they'd made love on the floor of the office-slash-studio. Siobhán had even joked about bringing a mattress in, but they'd settled on a large, comfortable armchair. It had seen plenty of use.

Now, Annie guided Siobhán toward it, steering her with her body. "What are you doing?" Siobhán said against her mouth, a hint of a smile in her voice.

"You'll just have to wait and see." When the back of Siobhán's knees hit the chair, Annie stopped. She reached down and lifted the soft, black cotton dress Siobhán wore, pulling it up and over her head. She unhooked the delicate cream and black lace bra, then slid the matching panties down over Siobhán's hips. "Very sexy," she murmured, planting a kiss on Siobhán's neck. "Were you planning this?"

Siobhán looped her arms around Annie's neck and let her head fall back. The long sweep of her hair brushed Annie's hands where they were clasped around Siobhán's waist. "I'm always planning this."

Laughing, Annie guided Siobhán down into the chair. "Well, then I guess I better make it good."

Siobhán paused and cupped Annie's cheek. "You always do, *álainn*. Always."

For a moment, they simply stared at each other. "Like you should talk. You are so, so beautiful," Annie said huskily. She planted a kiss on Siobhán's collarbone, nearly dizzy with the desire to taste Siobhán's skin. She was going to press Siobhán down against the cushions and bury her face between Siobhán's thighs until she came. Until she gorged herself on her lover. But for now, she simply looked at her, so overwhelmed by her feelings for Siobhán she could do nothing else.

Annie had never—would never—get enough of Siobhán Murray.

Annie and Siobhán's story will continue in "The Greenest Isle"

Book 2 in the "Colors" series

Brigham Vaughn

Brigham Vaughn is starting the adventure of a lifetime as a full-time writer. She devours books at an alarming rate and hasn't let her short arms and long torso stop her from doing yoga. She makes a killer key lime pie, hates green peppers, and loves wine tasting tours. A collector of vintage Nancy Drew books and green glassware, she enjoys poking around in antique shops and refinishing thrift store furniture. An avid photographer, she dreams of traveling the world and she can't wait to discover everything else life has to offer her.

Email: brighamvaughn@gmail.com
Facebook: www.facebook.com/brigham.vaughn
Facebook Author Page: www.facebook.com/pages/Author-Brigham-Vaughn/448104198635015
Facebook Fan Group (Brigham's Book Nerds):
www.facebook.com/groups/brighamsbooknerds/
Twitter: @AuthorBVaughn
G+: plus.google.com/+BrighamVaughn
Pinterest: www.pinterest.com/brighamvaughn/

Also by Brigham Vaughn

Pride Publishing (Totally Entwined Group)

StandaloneShort Stories
The Soldier Next Door (also part of the Right Here Right Now Anthology)

Tidal Series w/ K. Evan Coles (Novels)
Wake

Calm

Two Peninsulas Press (Self-Published)

Standalone Short Stories
Baby, It's Cold Inside

Geeks, Nerds, and Cuddles

Love in the Produce Aisle

Not So Suddenly

Sunburns and Sunsets

The French Toast Emergencies

The Wine Tasting Series (Short Stories)
Spit or Swallow

Aftertaste

Finish

Made in the USA
Columbia, SC
01 December 2017